# Jail
# Time

MIKE NEUN

Publishing Partners

Publishing Partners
Port Townsend, WA
www.marciabreece.com
marcia@marciabreece.com

Library of Congress Control Number: 2020910961

ISBN: 978-1-944887-57-5
eISBN: 978-1-944887-58-2

Interior layout: Marcia Breece
Cover design: Marcia Breece
eBook: Marcia Breece

Mike and Jintana

# CHAPTER 1

I WAS SITTING AT the front desk of my office when she walked in. She was not incredibly gorgeous in a slinky dress. No, she was in jeans, work boots, and a faded Pendleton shirt. You can't trust those detective novels. She looked to be in her late twenties, pleasant face, no makeup, brown hair cut short, great smile.

"I want you to solve a crime," she said.

"That's what I'm here for," said I, for I was indeed a private detective. I was also riding high, having solved a high-profile embezzlement case just three weeks ago. My client was now rolling in dough, had paid me handsomely, and was considering a run for the presidency.

Alas, his money manager was facing a few years behind bars.

"Tell me about the crime," I said.

"I can't do that. I haven't picked one."

"Oh, so you want me to solve a random crime."

"Yes. I want you to find a terrible criminal and take him down. There's too much evil in the world and I'd like to make one tiny dent. I just came into a pile of money, so I can pay."

"Really. How did you come into money?"

"There's this guy who hit it big and wants to build a huge houseboat on Lake Union. I got the job. It's exciting because he may run for president."

"Wow," I said. "Small world. So you want me to pick a bad guy, any bad guy, and take him out of action. Is this a MeToo thing? You want me to go after a sexual abuser?"

"I hadn't thought of that, but it might be a good crime. I'm a lesbian carpenter so sexual abuse hasn't been a problem for me. When you carry a hammer and nail gun people tend to leave you alone."

"That would be a deterrent. So you don't care what kind of criminal we choose."

"Nope. I just want you to destroy someone evil."

My ex-wife sprang to mind but I figured that was a little too close to home.

"Well, that doesn't narrow it down. There are a lot of evil people out there. Drug dealers, bank robbers, murderers, hedge fund operators, crooked cops . . . we've got a wide field to choose from."

"I'll tell you what," she said, "let's take a few days to think on it. I'm sure one of us can come up with some really horrible criminal and we can wipe him out. Or her. It doesn't have to be a guy."

"Okay, sounds like a plan."

"Do you need a retainer?"

"No, my teeth are straight."

She burst out laughing. "Do you always say that?"

"No, but I've always wanted to. Let's talk about money when we decide which crime to solve."

"If I pay extra can I help?"

"Only if you bring your nail gun. I don't want you out there unarmed."

She laughed. I liked this woman. Okay, she had weird ideas but so did I. Monte Grant III, private eye, had a new case.

"By the way," I said, "I should probably get your name."

"It's Lucy. My parents loved the Beatles."

"Ah yes, in the sky with diamonds."

"That's the one. Here's my card. Lucy George. You can always reach me at that number."

I took another look at her. She was certainly not slender, but she seemed strong, not fat. And her face was the same, with strong, pleasant features and that great smile. I realized this could be fun. Obviously, sex was off the table and I could use a friend.

I grabbed one of my cards from the little box on the desk and gave it to her.

"Here's mine, and that number's good anytime too. One more thing," I added. "This is not a whim, is it. There's a real reason you want to do this, right?"

She paused.

"Yes, there's a reason, and I don't want to talk about it."

"Fair enough."

"Do you drink beer?" she asked.

"Why yes I do. Dark beer if I can get it. Why do you ask?"

"Well, it's almost five o'clock and I figured your workday might be over. I'll buy you a beer if you buy the next."

"That sounds good," I said. "There's an Irish bar near here that has Guinness, and I've been known to drink that. Sound okay?"

"Does it have a pool table?"

"Why yes, I believe it does. Don't tell me you shoot pool."

She smiled. "I hope you don't get mad if a girl beats you."

"Nope, I just bump up the bet."

"Oh my," she said, "this could be interesting."

I closed up the office and we headed out to O'Reilly's.

# CHAPTER 2

THE NEXT DAY I was eating breakfast with Nails, the homeless ex-boxer who lives on the streets outside our building. I usually get us Egg McMuffins and coffee and we sit on the steps. It's better to eat outdoors because he doesn't smell that great and he sits three or four feet away because he knows it. I told him long ago I'd spring for an apartment but he's been on the streets for fifteen years and likes it. He's got a secret hideaway somewhere and I give him my old clothes so he stays warm.

"You're not looking good, boss," he says.

When a street person says you're not looking good, it's time to re-think your life choices.

"I had a rough night last night."

"Out with the boys?"

"No, out with a woman pool hustler. She plied me with Guinness and took me for a hundred bucks."

"She must've been good. I've seen you shoot pool and you're not easy money."

"Yeah, she was good. She was also intelligent, funny, and really not interested in men. What a waste."

"Maybe she's bisexual."

"I doubt it. She wears boots and a tool belt."

"That does sound kind of butch," said Nails. "How'd you end up with her?"

"She's a client."

"Whoa, that's great. You must be down to your last twenty million by now."

"I would be if I could get my hands on the money. Daddy set up an unbreakable trust fund."

"Poor you. Why the hell do you work?"

"It keeps me busy. By the way, I owe you for helping me on that last case."

"I didn't do much, just nosed around." Nails opened his ratty old overcoat. "I have this cloak of invisibility."

"Yeah, well you were a big help. What do you think, three hundred cover it?"

"Yeah, but don't give it to me here. Those other bums would rip me off in a heartbeat. Put it in my account."

Nails is a good beggar. Oh sure, he's a binge drinker but aside from that his expenses are about thirty cents a day. When he's not drunk he puts a few bucks into a bank account. It's a surprisingly healthy bank account because he's been doing it for years. I'll put the three hundred in later today.

We finished our McMuffins.

"So," he said, "what's the case?"

"Well, that's the weird part. She wants me to pick a crime and solve it."

"Any crime?"

"Yep. Any crime at all. She just wants to bring down some really bad guy. You have any candidates?"

"Well there are some slimeballs out there but let me think awhile. Tell me more about this lady."

"Her name is Lucy George and she's a contractor. She's going to build this mega houseboat on Lake Union for a rich guy so she'll have some extra cash. By the way, you know the rich guy. He was our last client."

"No shit. Our next president?"

"God, I hope not. He'd be a disaster."

"You got that right. So Lucy wants to bring down a criminal mastermind."

Nails' brow furrowed.

"Well, we've got a lot to choose from," he said. "Maybe we should make a list."

"My plan exactly. If you think of any names, let me know. I've got to get to the office now. You good for Saturday choir?"

"Yep."

MY FRIENDS LAUGHED at my choir idea. I'd had a band in high school and still played guitar but I couldn't play lead and my singing was marginal. My rock and roll dreams had fallen by the wayside, so I thought, *why not get a bunch of street people and sing?* We could probably bring in more money than they could make begging and split the take, so every Saturday our motley group meets at Pike Place Market. The numbers vary, the quality is low, but we have fun and always make money. Ha! Take that, ye of little faith.

"And breakfast tomorrow?"

"See you here."

He wandered off. I picked up the wrappers and coffee cups and threw them in the trash basket. Then I walked into Grant Tower, greeted Willie at the high desk across from the glass entrance, walked across the marble lobby floor and pushed the elevator button.

# CHAPTER 3

BERNADETTE WAS AT her desk. Thirty-two years old, tall, in jeans and a Harley tee shirt, black hair, she was a handsome woman once you got past the tattoos and piercings. She looked up from the computer and I realized, uh oh, once Lucy caught sight of her, I was going to be odd man out. I had no doubt Bernadette had tried everything and gay sex was probably high on the list. Monte Grant III, matchmaker.

"Hi boss," she said.

"Hi Bernadette. You all caught up?"

"Yep. Not much to it. Paid the bills, cashed the checks, we've got money in the bank and I paid myself."

"Did you give yourself a bonus?"

"Why would I do that?"

"Because we've got money in the bank and you've got kids. Make it a good one."

"Hell, I can make it a great one."

"Whatever's fair, but if it's too much I'll have to go back to working alone."

She gave me a number. I added more and she smiled happily.

Bernadette is a single mom with two young kids and she comes in whenever she can. I don't need a real secretary because it would be silly to have someone waiting for the phone not to ring.

Sometimes when her ex-boyfriend is in town, she brings the kids to the office and turns it into a daycare center. Her ex is a mean bastard and my office is safe because he has no idea she works here. His stage name is Dread and he's a bass player for a struggling thrash metal band. Apparently nobody told them their music is forty years out of date. They play biker bars and grungy saloons and Dread fits right in. Lots of tattoos, whiskey drinker, drug connection, lover of brawls—he was not exactly boyfriend material.

Why do women love outlaws? I will never understand that. Oh sure, Bernadette had been a biker too, with her own chopper until she'd sold it to buy cocaine—always a good business decision. And yes, she'd served time in the joint after a fight with another biker chick.

I have Nails to thank for Bernadette. He'd heard about her situation from an ex-biker on the streets and asked me to give her a chance. Surprisingly, she was intelligent and knew computers, so I hired her. It was one of the best moves I ever made.

I noticed her toddlers playing in the conference room. The twin boys are two now and surprisingly, not terrible. How can a biker chick and thrash metal bass player produce two quiet kids? Humans are weird.

"I take it Dread is in town?"

"Yeah. One of my old girlfriends warned me."

"Does he ever mess with your apartment?"

"He hasn't yet. Actually, I hope he does 'cause I've got cameras set up. Should've done that years ago. I could've put him away for domestic assault. Now if he screws with the apartment, I can get him for breaking and entering, malicious violence."

"Wow, you've gone all legal on me."

"Amazing what you can learn working for a big-time private eye."

"Okay, you and the kids can stay here as long as you want. You need beds?"

"No. I've got a couple air mattresses and it's like camping out. They like it here."

"Did I tell you we've got a new client?"

"No shit. Two in one month? You must be exhausted."

"I think I can bear up. Our client's a bit strange but she's going to be interesting."

"She?"

"Yeah. She's a carpenter and very butch."

"Sounds hot. After Dread I'm ready to switch teams. When do I get to meet her?"

"In a couple of days. Start up a file for Lucy George."

"Wow, she's even got girl-boy names. That's kind of a tipoff isn't it? What's the crime?"

"We haven't decided yet."

I told her Lucy's plan.

"That's it. Know any vicious criminals?"

"Well, Dread springs to mind but he's just minor bad. I know bikers who'd make him look like a juvie. You just want thugs or something higher? A criminal mastermind? A third-world dictator?"

"I'm not sure we could bring down a dictator, but it would be fun wouldn't it? A big feather in our cap."

"Yeah, but it might be beyond our capabilities."

"Right." I said. "We're a bit short on mercenaries and tactical weapons. Let's try to come up with someone bigger than a biker, smaller than a dictator."

We're both good with computers. Too good, really, because she'd run some scams with the bikers and I'd wasted my youth as a gamer. I told her to see what she could find and I'd check my sources. By my sources I meant Nails. When you grow up in country clubs and yachting circles you don't really connect with gangsters. Financial crimes? Yes. I'm sure I met some Bernie Madoffs in my time, but murderous, sadistic criminals? Probably not. Being a private eye was a steep learning curve.

I went into my office and gently lifted one of the toddlers off my chair. He didn't take it well and started screaming. I'm not stupid. I put him back on the chair and went over and sat on the sofa. I didn't really have anything to do so I picked up my Walter Mosley book and did some more research into private detecting. The other toddler untied my shoes. He thought it was funny. I pretended to be mad. He thought that was funnier.

I tried to figure out what kind of crime I wanted to solve. At the top of my list would be any crime that involved kids but I didn't know if I could handle that kind of trauma. I can understand crimes of anger or greed, but hurting a kid? That just sickened me. Would I want to spend weeks dealing with that? No. And yet, maybe those crimes are the ones that are the most need of solving. Damn. This wasn't easy. My biggest hope was that Lucy, Nails or Bernadette would come up with something and get me off the hook.

I brewed up some espresso and sat back on the sofa watching the two boys play with Nerf balls. We should have Nerf crime. No harm, no foul. Why don't gangsters listen to me? You know how coffee is supposed to keep you awake? Not me. I finished my espresso and drifted off to sleep on the sofa.

# CHAPTER 4

I WOKE UP GROGGY from a dream where Nazis were taking over the city and putting Nerf criminals in concentration camps. I also realized the toddlers were zonked out on the carpet, so apparently this nap thing is contagious. Nazis? They commit crimes. Race crimes . . . hate crimes . . . that could be the way to go. Call me old fashioned, but I never liked Nazis, or neo-Nazis, and realized they'd jumped to the top of my list. They'd grown more active lately, even in Seattle, and I knew there were clusters of them in our city. As a rich white guy, I'm sure I could work undercover. Hey, didn't rich white guys finance Hitler? On the other hand, I wasn't fond of tattoos and I'd never seen a neo-Nazi without them. I didn't think I'd go for a big swastika on my chest. It could hurt my standing at the country club.

Anyway, it was a possibility and I did what any smart person would do. I googled Seattle, neo-Nazis. I would've had Bernadette do it but I realized some of them might've been friends of hers when she was a biker. No sense getting her upset.

At that moment she walked in. I know, psychic hotline.

"Boss," she said, "can you watch the kids? I want to go to a meeting."

Mine is a full-service office building. I hadn't known it but A.A. had meetings in a conference room on the third floor. It was an accounting firm and apparently all those numbers can drive you to drink. Bernadette attended regularly.

"Sure," I said, "no problem." When they woke up we could play the shoelace game.

I went back to my search and found bikers and Nazis were deeply involved. Bullies in arms. Ah yes, bullies. This brought memories of the biggest problem in my young life—nasty guys who made life miserable for kids like me.

My parents were very rich and very liberal, kind of a rare combination, and their plan was put me in public schools. None of this prep school bullshit for their kid. I was a lousy athlete, wore thick glasses and was a gamer—a prime target for bullies. I got punched, wedgied, stuck in lockers, all the classic moves and there was no way I was going to fight back because I would've gotten killed. I'm weak but I'm not stupid.

So I had to find other answers and a computer was my weapon of choice. I became the high school spy. Monte Grant III, scourge of the underworld.

My biggest takedown was the captain of the football team, Pete Downey. He was our star fullback, about 235 pounds of muscle, and a mean son of a bitch. You know those old school parents who say if someone picks on you, you should hit back? Those parents are idiots. Big Pete would've put me in traction. Instead, I sneaked out at night and followed him around trying to find anything weird. Social media would've been a big help but it hadn't been invented yet. On the other hand, I had a Sony Handicam and a Dell computer.

One night I was in the bushes outside his house when I saw his parents leave. I sneaked up to the window and there was Pete, just watching TV. Nothing. But I was on a mission and I was patient. In awhile he got up and walked over to the liquor cabinet. I started taking video. He jimmied the door, got a bottle of vodka and took it back to the couch. I got it recorded, but it wasn't all that scandalous.

Next he got up, turned off the TV, and left the room. He came back with a sex magazine and a washcloth and I knew this was going to be golden. I got fifteen minutes of him whacking off and realized that for a big guy he had a pretty small dick. Perfect.

We had an exchange student from England and he'd taught us all the word, "wanker." What a great word! My anonymous floppy discs went viral and for the rest of his time in high school, Pete was known as "Wanker" and "Little Peter." It was a cruel, cruel thing I'd done and it didn't bother me a bit. I hope it destroyed his love life. Monte Grant III, super spy, strikes again.

So, my first picks for bad guys were wanker bullies or neo-Nazis, but maybe Lucy, Bernadette and Nails had better ideas. Bernadette asked if she and the boys could stay camped out in the conference room and I said sure. I have two conference rooms and never use either of them, so why not? Then I ordered some Thai food and we had a picnic. I left as she was setting up the air mattresses and took the elevator up to my home. It also has rooms I never use, but hey, it's my building.

# CHAPTER 5

NAILS AND I SAT on the steps munching our McMuffins and I recognized some of his clothes. I give him my old clothes, clean, and two hours later they look like he's been mud wrestling. I don't know how he does that.

"You come up with any criminal masterminds?" he asked.

"Yeah. I had one thought but I don't know how good it is."

"A good crime?"

"More a selection of criminals," I said. "What do you know about neo-Nazis?"

"Ooooh, good idea Boss. I know they like to beat up street people. I had a couple friends get roughed up by skinheads. It wasn't pretty."

"You ever get messed with?" I asked.

"Once. I guess they didn't expect me to be a fighter."

"Must've been a surprise."

"It was. They started giving me shit, pushing me around, and I got the first guy with a left hook before he knew he was even in a fight. Bam! Laid him out. The second guy was pretty big so I worked the body. Funny how all that stuff comes back to you. He took a couple shots to the stomach, dropped his guard and bam, right cross."

"Knockout?"

"Down for the count."

"What'd you do then?"

"Walked away. What do you think? Call the cops? There weren't any witnesses and they'd have arrested me for assault."

"Yeah, I guess you're right."

We munched our McMuffins.

You ever think about the old days?" I asked.

"In the ring? Sometimes. I wasn't that bad. Had some good fights, made some good money, got ripped off by my manager, the usual story."

"Wish I'd been around. Think I would've made a good manager?"

"Well, you wouldn't have had to rip me off. It's not like you needed my money. But boxing is filled with some scary characters. I don't think you would've lasted."

"I don't know," I said. "Sometimes I surprise people."

"Sometimes I do too. Those skinheads didn't know what hit 'em."

I wondered how old Nails was. He looked fifty or sixty but street life ages people. He had a missing tooth. Did I mention he's black? Surprise, a black fighter who gets ripped off by a manager. When does that ever happen? His hair was ratty, and so was his beard. I wondered what he'd look like cleaned up. I'd offered everything—a room, a shower, a haircut and shave—but he wanted no part of it. I wished I were smarter, smart enough to get him back together. Obviously, I wasn't.

"Well," I said, "how about you? Any bad guys? How about those assholes in boxing? Managers? Promoters?"

"It would be fun," he said, "and I know some that could use time in the slammer, but I think we can do better. We can find people who are more evil than that."

"Got any in mind?"

"Well," he said, "I never liked pimps but they're small fry. Trafficking is worse. You wouldn't believe what those guys do to girls. I wouldn't mind bringing down one of them."

"I hadn't thought of that," I said. "Good idea. Okay, we've got a couple of possibles to run past Lucy and we'll see what she's come up with. I feel like the Lone Ranger."

"I'm with you Kemosabe," said Nails. "Silver bullets and all that shit."

"Truth, justice and the American way."

"Isn't that superman?"

"Oops. My bad. Got my heroes mixed up."

He got up and wandered off to hustle spare change. I gathered the wrappers and coffee cups and took them over to the trash bin. It was a good start to the day. I turned, walked up the steps to the heavy glass doors of my building and headed in.

I'd inherited this building from my dad. He'd gotten his money the old-fashioned way, as a Wall Street pirate. Rigging futures markets, insider trading, false rumors—he'd used all the tools. Then he and his wife—not my mom, she was long gone and this was three wives later—were killed in a yachting accident. We liked to call it an accident, but the truth was one of the millionaires he'd destroyed had made his money in construction and demolition. He loaded a cigarette boat with dynamite and became the world's first ex-millionaire suicide bomber. Drove that speedboat into my dad's yacht at sixty miles per hour with the explosives going off on impact. They say the largest piece of either boat was about the size of a shingle.

I was invited to the reading of the will and looked upon with scorn by the relatives. I'd flunked out of Harvard—hard to do when your father put big money into the endowment—and joined the Coast Guard. Hey, boats run in the family. I served modestly for five years, got out and failed as a ski instructor, real estate developer, restaurant manager, independent film maker, stand-up comedian and a bunch of other endeavors. These were financial disasters, but nothing my trust fund couldn't handle.

I finally became a private detective because I'd read every Robert B. Parker novel and thought, I could do that!

The reading of Dad's will was classic. Drama, hate, outrage, tears—it had it all. Once you start with the fact that Dad had blown all the money and was on his yacht fleeing to Grand Cayman, you can imagine the howls of anger. Then you get to where the only asset he still owned was Grant Tower, the sixteen-story office building in downtown Seattle, and that he bequeathed it to me, the place became completely unglued. I was physically attacked by three ex-wives and a couple of cousins. Thank God security showed up.

Luckily the lawyers didn't mention that my trust fund was untouchable and still intact, giving me a yearly income in the high six figures. If they had, the relatives would've formed a militia. When they eventually did find out there were actual death threats. Later on I helped out the ones I liked, under the table. The ones I didn't like? The hell with them.

Why did Dad give me the building? It turned out I was the only family member who hadn't tried to hustle him for money, leverage, stock tips, or whatever.

Also, Dad and I had a great relationship. We'd get together every couple of months and get roaring drunk in a sleazy bar. Our goal was to give the people who worked there the best night of their lives and we wildly over-tipped, bought drinks for the world, laughed, and blasted each other with insults for hours. I loved my dad and I guess he loved me. Deep down I knew he was a crook and wouldn't trust him around my money or any woman I really liked. I wasn't stupid.

So I got a building, with enough rent coming in to cover taxes, maintenance, and improvements. I don't have to work but I get easily bored so I opened my new business as a private eye. I liked it.

# CHAPTER 6

"NAILS," I SAID, as we sat on the steps, "I'd like you to be in on this case right from the start but we have a problem."

"What's that?"

"Well, there are four of us. You, me, Lucy and Bernadette. I'd like to work as a team, which means we'll have to meet together."

"Ah . . ." he said, the light dawning, "like in a room?"

"Yes. In a room."

"And I'm dirty and smell bad."

"Right. I know you like your life and you've proved you don't want help from me, but if you want in on this project you may have to change your lifestyle."

"But then I won't be as useful on the street. Do you want to sacrifice that?"

"Good point. Can you switch back and forth? Clean up for any time we have to work together and go street person to gather information?"

He thought about that.

"You know I won't give up my life."

"I know you won't. It's your decision."

He thought some more.

"We're talking showers, right? And clean clothes? The works?"

"Right. I know it's a lot to ask."

"What if I want to get down and dirty and go on a binge?"

"Lord knows I can't stop you. That's your call."

"You drive a hard bargain, Monte. Okay, I'll do it for this project, but don't get your hopes up. I will go back to the streets."

"Agreed. So let's go up to the penthouse and get you cleaned up."

We walked into the building. Willie at the front desk raised his eyebrows but I waved him off. I almost passed out from the stench on the ride up the elevator, but we made it and I led him directly to the shower. He took a forty-five-minute shower and I worried that might not be enough. While he was in there I took his old clothes down to the dumpster and laid out some of mine. We were close enough to the same size, both slender and just under six feet tall. Lucky.

When he came out he said, "These clothes suck. Don't you have any jeans? I feel like a pimp."

Actually he looked quite good in slacks, a button-down shirt and loafers. His hair and beard were still a little matted, but they were clean. I gave him a toothbrush and some toiletries and waited outside while he finished up. I realized that in his youth Nails must've been a handsome dude and even now with his slightly broken nose and scarring over the eyebrows, he was still a good-looking guy. I couldn't understand his choices, but I'd learned years ago I could never change people. They are what they are.

We took the elevator down one floor to my office and I made a mental note to have the elevator cleaned. The smell lingered.

We met in my other conference room. As I said, I have way too much space, but what the hell.

We walked into the room and found Bernadette and

Lucy talking like old chums. I love strong women, but with them I realized I might be overdoing it. It occurred to me that either one could take me in a fight. I Introduced Nails and was happy to see him act quite courtly with the ladies. He shook their hands gently and said he was pleased to meet them. I'd prepared Lucy and Bernadette for a street person, so they were pleasantly surprised to meet this black gentleman.

We all sat down and I opened up our first meeting.

"Okay," I said, "we all know the score. Lucy wants to pay us to find a really nasty criminal and take him down. Everyone okay with that?"

Nails nodded and Bernadette answered, "I'm fine as long as my kids are safe."

Lucy turned to her. "You've got kids?"

"Yes," said Bernadette. "Toddlers, twin boys."

"Oh man that's great, when can I meet them? How old are they?"

"They're two and I'll take you to meet them after our meeting."

"What am I?" asked Nails, "Chopped liver? Don't I get to meet the kids?"

"Of course," said Bernadette. "They'll be waking up from their nap in an hour or so."

"Are they okay alone?"

"Yeah. We set up the other conference room like a playroom. They sleep on a big air mattress so if they roll out of bed it's about a three-inch fall. I've got a baby monitor too, in my purse."

"Wow," said Lucy. "You are a mother. I'm impressed."

I interrupted.

"I hate to bother you all, but shouldn't we be holding this meeting?"

Lucy turned to me and started singing the old song, "We believe the children are the future . . . ."

We laughed.

"Okay, okay. I stand corrected. How are those kids doing Bernadette?"

She laughed and we got down to business.

"We've all had time to come up with ideas. Lucy, this is your deal, so what are your thoughts?"

"I tried to pick out someone evil," Lucy said, "but it seems like the world is full of bad people. Way too many choices."

"You got that, sister," said Bernadette, "it's a jungle out there. I tried to narrow it down but I could name you a hundred assholes who deserve to be taken out."

"This is Seattle," I said, "so it's not like we're dealing with the mafia. In New York or Detroit or Chicago you'd know who the crime families are and you could just go after one of the capos. Seattle seems like a clean town compared to those places."

"Don't kid yourself, Boss," said Nails, "Seattle's a big city and every big city has crime. We got gangs, drive-bys, turf wars. We got all the crimes every city has. On top of that, it's a port. So there's human trafficking, drugs, smuggling, hijacking, all kinds of crime. For one thing, the Asian gangs could be worse than the mafia. Those guys are vicious."

"Okay," I said, "we have lots of choices. Other ideas?"

Bernadette spoke up. "Do we work close to home or would it be smarter to go far away so it doesn't get traced back to us?"

"I like the idea," said Nails, "mostly because I'd like to stay alive when this is done. But that means we have to travel and travel doubles the risk unless we're going to shoot the guy. Are we going to shoot the guy?"

We all looked doubtful.

"How about this," I said, "let's pick out our target first. Maybe that'll help us decide how to deal with him. By the way, I'm not ruling out women. There are definitely some evil women out there too."

"Right, Boss," said Bernadette. "I met some in prison who would be perfect targets."

"You were in prison?" said Lucy, astonished.

"Yeah," said Bernadette, "it was a bar fight that got out of hand. The bitch attacked me and I went a little crazy. Stomped her."

"You killed her?"

"No, nothing like that. Just broke a couple ribs. I was wearing boots. She would've done the same to me. Biker chicks are like that."

"Wow," said Lucy. "And I thought I was a macho carpenter. You don't seem like that kind of person."

"Well, drugs had a lot to do with it, and a mean boyfriend. It all came together and I exploded. Too bad for that chick in the bar."

"Again," I said, "we seem to be veering off track. We have to pick out a target."

"Right, Boss, sorry about that. Back to business."

Just then we heard kid noises from her purse.

"Oh shit, the boys are awake. I've got to go check on them."

"I want to see them," said Lucy. "We can talk later can't we?"

I knew when I was beaten. Besides, I hated meetings.

We trooped out through the office and back into the other conference room/playroom/bedroom. The kids were up but still a little groggy from their nap. They lit up when they saw the four of us come in and soon we were all on the floor playing with them. I'm not great with kids so I mostly watched as Lucy, Bernadette and Nails wrestled, laughed, cuddled and played with the boys. Nails surprised me. He was perfectly comfortable with them and they with him.

I sent out for pizza and we ate it sitting on the floor and talking while the kids roamed around, happy to have new people to play with. I realized this was one of the best afternoons of my life, eating pizza, playing with kids, hanging out with Bernadette, Nails and Lucy. I'm not big on socializing, but this was amazingly comfortable. Somewhere there were people in country clubs or out on yachts and I didn't envy them a bit.

# CHAPTER 7

AFTER DINNER BERNADETTE and Lucy talked while Nails and I played with the boys. I was getting better with them once I found I could just join in on whatever they wanted to do. Bernadette asked Lucy how she'd gotten into the construction business.

"My dad was a carpenter," she said. "He did remodels and worked construction but he never made a lot of money. He had a shop in the basement and I loved to follow him around. I'd go down and hand him tools and eventually he showed me how they worked and let me try them out. Soon I became a pretty good woodworker. My mom hated it."

"Ah yes," said Bernadette. "She wanted you to be a girly girl, right?"

"Yeah, she would've liked me to go shopping with her and play with makeup, all that stuff. I was never into it, but I tried for her sake."

"What about boys?"

"They just seemed kind of silly. I tried to like them but I never really did. Did you?"

"Oh hell yes," said Bernadette. "Too much. I got in all kinds of trouble. I liked bad boys and you know where that leads. Sex, drugs and rock and roll."

"Uh oh."

"Yeah. Next thing I knew I was a biker chick with a violent boyfriend and a cocaine habit."

"That's sad."

"Well, there were good times too. I loved riding choppers. But back to you. When did you find out you were a lesbian?"

"Oh I think I always knew. But there was a lot of pressure to be one of the girls. I didn't come out until I got to college. You know what's funny? In college there was almost as much pressure to be a lesbian as there was to be straight. People are weird."

"Wow. College. I only had a year at community college. I hated school but I loved the parties."

"They were good, but I liked the classes too. I took civil engineering, architecture, electrical engineering, all the dorky guy stuff. Summers I went back to Sandpoint and worked construction with my dad. Mostly remodels but we built some houses too. It was great."

"And after college?"

"Some friends and I worked around town, doing carpentry, construction, we even worked on some boats. Eventually I started my own little company. I've got two guys and three women working for me."

"You get to boss guys around? I'd like that."

"Yeah I do. It takes awhile but once they find out I know what I'm doing things work out okay."

Around eight o'clock the boys got sleepy and Bernadette bedded them down in the corner. Then we sat on the other side of the room and talked in low tones.

"Okay," I said, "we've all had time to think about targets. Nails?"

"I hate pimps," said Nails, "because they prey on homeless girls, but if you go higher, you could take down one of those traffickers who preys on lots of women."

Lucy and Bernadette nodded, obviously pleased with that one.

"Okay," I said. "Bernadette, what have you come up with?"

"Well," she said, "when I was a biker, we dealt meth up and down the I-5 corridor. That shit destroys people and I wouldn't mind taking out the guys who produce it. It's not that hard to find a meth lab and it's easy to blow it up. My other thought is when I was in prison (I don't think Lucy had come to grips with that yet. Who was this chick?) all the girls talked about this one judge who was evil. He had a hard-on for women criminals and handed down outrageous sentences. There were girls in there doing hard time for minor offenses and it was awful. I'd like to take him out."

"Works for me," I said. "Good. We've got some candidates. Lucy?"

"This is off the wall," she said, "but I know a developer who's going to kill people. Not like a criminal but like a corrupt bastard who's building stuff out of cheap materials and someday they're going to fail. In five or ten years one decent tremor will shake them to pieces. To me, it's like mass murder waiting to happen. I am so pissed."

"Another good candidate," I said.

"What about you, boss?" asked Bernadette. "Any evil people in your country-club set?"

"Lots of 'em," I replied, "but it's mostly financial crime and corruption. I tried to think outside the box and realized the people I hate most are neo-Nazis. They're evil, they terrorize people who can't fight back, and I'd love to take one of their top guys down."

The two women nodded.

"Okay," said Bernadette. "We've got candidates. The next question is, how do we take them down? Are we vigilantes? Do we do a Dirty Harry and shoot them? Do we spy on them, collect evidence and turn them in?"

"I can't shoot anyone," I said. "I hate guns and I'm not Charles Bronson."

"Who's Charles Bronson?" asked Lucy.

I felt really old.

"He was a movie tough guy, one of my favorites."

"Ah," she said, "like Vin Diesel."

I was about to ask who Vin Diesel was but wisely refrained. I hate being laughed at.

"Anyway," I said, "I can't shoot anyone."

"Same here," said Lucy. "I'm tough, but not killer tough. I was thinking more along the lines of bringing them to justice."

"Well," said Bernadette, "in the old days I could've killed my boyfriend but now that I've cleaned up and have kids I don't think I can do it either."

I turned to Nails.

"What about it?"

"Count me out too," he said. "I think if I was pushed really hard I might lose it and kill someone, but in cold blood? I don't think I could do it."

"Okay," I said. "Actually, that's a big relief. I don't even want to be around shooting or stabbing. I'd hate to faint in front of you guys."

We talked some more but didn't really come up with either a hard target or a plan. There was no hurry, and after awhile Lucy said she was beat and was going home to get some sleep.

We decided to meet in the morning and I convinced Nails it would be stupid to get all homeless for one night only to come back and shower again. I had a spare bedroom in the penthouse—actually I had two more but who's counting—and if a bed was against his street code he could always throw blankets on the floor and sleep there. Reluctantly, he agreed. We adjourned for the night.

# CHAPTER 8

LUCY HAD TO WORK the next morning, so we put off the meeting until nap time for the kids.

That afternoon Lucy was again dressed in jeans, a work shirt and boots. All she needed was a hard hat and I'm sure she had one in her truck. How did I know she had a truck? I'm psychic.

Bernadette wore jeans too, with her favorite Harley tee shirt. Call me crazy, but aren't detectives supposed to be surrounded by hot chicks in slinky outfits? Aren't these knockouts always supposed to be putting moves on him instead of each other? How did this go so terribly wrong? Oh well, I liked them both and with Nails I felt we had a good team. Weird, maybe, but good.

Lucy started.

"We all agreed we're not going to go full vigilante, right? No bursting into rooms killing people."

We agreed, but Nails looked a little wistful. Hard to believe a prizefighter didn't yearn for the violent solution.

"So, we're left with the spying, gathering of evidence solution, right? Or is there another way?"

There was a long pause while we thought about that.

Bernadette broke the silence.

"When I was with Dread . . . , she started.

"Hold it right there," said Lucy. "Dread?"

"Yeah, stupid name, right? He was a biker and a bass player in a thrash metal band. Slash was his hero and he wanted a one-word stage name. He picked Dread."

"Didn't he know it's been taken? Judge Dredd?"

"No one accused him of being a genius. Anyway, when I was with him some of us bikers kidnapped a guy. Got him alone, threw him in a van and took him to an abandoned factory. He was a rat, sold out some of our guys to the cops, and we needed to know who put him up to it."

"What happened then?" asked Nails.

"He told us."

"Why did he tell you?"

"I don't want to go into that," said Bernadette. "I still have nightmares. Those biker dudes were vicious and I had to get out of there. They called me a pussy and I guess I was."

"Naw," said Nails. "You just weren't an animal."

"I got arrested pretty soon after that and you know what? I was relieved. It was a way of getting out of that whole horror film."

"So the kids in the next room have a father named Dread?" said Lucy.

"Who knows? Whoever had blow could've been the father. I just hope biker genes aren't hereditary."

Lucy, the tough construction boss, looked like she was going to cry. Nails looked angry. I felt like the biggest preppy rich boy dilettante who ever lived.

"Back to the story," said Nails. "What happened to the guy, the one they kidnapped?"

"He disappeared. That's all I want to know. I didn't see him die."

Again, there was a silence.

"Okay," I said, "we haven't considered kidnapping the

bad guy. It's pretty far fetched but if we did it, what would we do with him?"

"I have no idea," said Bernadette. "But I vote against torture and killing."

"Hold on a minute," said Lucy. "Did any of you hear about that black dude who made friends with KKK members and turned them around? I saw a YouTube thing about him. He's a musician and a writer."

"Not me," said Nails. "I don't think that story made it into the homeless grapevine."

"I might've seen something," I said, "but I don't remember much. Didn't they make a movie about him?"

"Maybe," said Lucy. "It was hard to believe. He went to interview this KKK leader and didn't tell the guy he was black. Somehow, he got the guy talking and it went on from there. He fucking converted a KKK guy! Then he converted some others."

"It sounds like his plan was way better than ours," I said. "He mixed with evil dudes and took out the evil. That is awesome."

Nails looked thoughtful.

"What if . . ." he said and paused. "What if we kidnapped our criminal and figured out a way to get to him? What if we didn't torture him, or kill him, but turned him around?"

"It's a great idea, but I don't think we have the skills," I said.

"I bet that KKK whisperer didn't think he had the skills either, and he's only one guy. Maybe with the four of us coming at him we could figure out a way."

"This is almost religious," said Bernadette. "We're talking about saving souls here. Are we thinking we're some sort of saint? I know for a fact I'm way on the other side of that scale."

I was intrigued. This was a truly crazy idea and I love crazy ideas. I looked around the table and realized my strange crew did too. Could we actually get to an evil person? Turn him inside out? Would it take years? Then I had a thought that was even more weird.

"We haven't considered the possibility that he could turn us! Instead of us converting him into a decent person he could turn us into evil ones. These big-time gangsters are masters at manipulation, probably better than we are. Instead of saving his soul, he could take ours! We're talking Satan here. Ultimate evil versus people who aren't saints."

"I boxed Satan once," said Nails. "Knocked him out."

We stared.

"Yeah," he said, "there was this crazy Detroit boxer, called himself Satan. Wore red trunks, red robe, had smoke machines when he entered the ring. Even had his canine teeth sharpened. Weird-looking dude and crazy as a bedbug. But it worked. He drew big crowds and they put him up against a bunch of stiffs so he had a good record. I wasn't high ranked but I wasn't a stiff. His people didn't know that. Fought him in a New Jersey casino. Big crowd. Satan versus Nails Norrison. The trouble was, he dropped his right. Not a lot, but enough. In the fourth round he jabbed, started to throw the right, and I came over the top with a left hook. Boom! End of Satan. I felt bad about it, because it was a good gimmick and I cost him a lot of money. But it felt good to take on the devil and beat him. One punch, laid him out."

"Wow," said Lucy, "great story. So you were a good fighter?"

"Yeah," Nails laughed. "I coulda been a champion."

"Really?"

"Naw. There were guys who were faster. Better. I was good but not great and there's a huge difference."

"But you beat Satan!"

"Yeah," he smiled. "I beat Satan."

"Maybe we can too," she said, wistfully.

It was an idiotic plan. But it was all we had. We just needed a target and that was proving difficult. Luckily the kids woke up and we didn't have to deal with it anymore. As I said, I hate meetings.

We played with them awhile and then Lucy got up to leave and Nails did too.

"Where are you going?" I asked him.

"Sorry, Boss, I'm getting claustrophobic. I gotta get back out on the streets. Gotta let the guys know I'm still around. Some of them sorta depend on me."

"What are you going to do for clothes? I threw out your old stuff."

"You got any old jeans and tee shirts? Maybe a jacket?"

I thought.

"I don't think I do. I never wear that kind of stuff."

"I do," said Lucy. "I've got lots of beat up stuff I wore on the job sites. I'm a little smaller than you but they're baggy and should work. Come on, we'll head over to my house and we'll fix you up, then I'll drive you back downtown."

Nails looked at me. I nodded and smiled, and he followed Lucy out the door.

"I like them," said Bernadette.

"I do too," I said. "I don't know what's going to come of all this but I like all of you."

"The kids like them too. I trust their judgement better than mine."

"Makes sense. I've seen some of your choices."

We laughed.

"Okay," she said. "I've been thinking of going back to my apartment tomorrow. I haven't seen or heard anything from Dread, so maybe it's okay."

"Let's think about it. Better safe than sorry."

"Okay Boss. Sweet dreams."

I waved good night and headed upstairs.

# CHAPTER 9

NAILS AND I SAT on the steps eating our health food Egg McMuffins and I was amazed to find he'd managed to regain street person filthiness in just under fifteen hours.

"How do you do that?" I asked.

"Do what?"

"Get that dirty so fast? You're like a little kid wallowing in a bog."

"Years of practice," he said. "We street people have an image to uphold. If I walked around clean, I'd be a discredit to my people."

"Lucy's going to hate what you've done to her clothes."

"Oh she was going to throw these away. She just hadn't gotten around to it. I like her. We had a nice talk in her truck."

Bingo. I knew she had a truck.

"I hate to break it to you, but we're having another meeting this afternoon. You'll have to shower again."

"Oh no, boss. This is harassment. I'll have to talk to human resources. Forced cleanliness is a crime against humanity."

"Sue me. Better yet, sue Lucy and Bernadette. We're doing it for them."

"Yeah, but they're not rich. I'm going for the

deep pockets."

"Nails?"

"Yeah boss."

"How come you don't talk like a boxer?"

"You think I should throw in some 'dees' and 'does', get real black?"

"You have to admit, you don't sound like you come from the hood."

"Boss, this is Seattle. There is no hood. People think there is, but we're not talking Compton here. I didn't come from the projects."

"Where did you come from?"

"Garfield. My parents were teachers. Mom taught grade school, Dad taught math."

"I bet they were thrilled when you told them you wanted to be a boxer."

"Whoa. The shit hit the fan that night! I was a decent student, supposed to go to UW, make the family proud. I didn't even tell them I'd been fighting amateur for two years. Mom cried, Dad got mad, the other kids ran and hid. It was a big night in the Norrison household."

"They let you do it?"

"No, they forbid it. So I ran away from home. Later on we talked, but they never got over it. By the time everything went to hell my parents were old. They wanted to help, but they were just scraping by themselves. Teachers don't make a lot of money and they had four kids."

"How'd the other kids do?"

"Much better. My brother joined the Air Force, became a pilot. My little sisters did okay too. One's a radiation technician, the other is teaching high school. So the parents got three out of four."

"You ever go see your parents?"

"Oh hell yes. I drive my Mercedes over to their house in

Greenlake and impress them with my grooming."

"Sorry. Bad question."

"Yeah, I dropped out of society, family, all that stuff."

We paused, sipping coffee. And then he started chuckling.

"What?"

"I just solved our problem. About which criminal to pick."

"Really."

"Sure. It's obvious. We just find a neo-Nazi biker meth dealer crooked judge who's a human trafficker."

I laughed.

"Brilliant. You sure you were a boxer? Sure you didn't graduate in logic?"

"Yeah, I kept it a secret all these years." He laughed. "No, I learned all my logic in the ring. Simple stuff. Don't get hit, look for a weakness, never trust a manager. That's about it."

"Got it. Okay we'll meet again when the kids are napping. Come on up and take a shower about 2:30."

"I'm calling my lawyer. Cleanliness is slavery."

He walked away. I picked up the wrappers and cups and threw them in the trash bin. Then I headed up to the office.

# CHAPTER 10

I WALKED IN, gave Bernadette a cheerful hello and realized she didn't answer. I looked closer and saw she was close to crying. I'd never seen her cry and didn't think it was possible. She was the toughest person I'd ever known. I stopped in front of her desk.

"What happened?"

"Dread knows I'm here."

"How?"

"Some dude saw me come in the building and told him."

"Damn. But it's no big deal, he can't get up here. Security would stop him."

"I know, but it also means I can't go out. He's out there somewhere and he texted me he's going to mess me up if he catches me in the streets."

"You got the text?"

"No, he deleted it as soon as he saw I read it."

"So you're wacko ex-boyfriend is down there somewhere waiting to mess you up if you go outside."

"Yeah. I can't even go get things for the kids. I need food and diapers and stuff."

"No problem there. Write down what you need and I'll go get it."

"You can't do that. You're the boss. I'm supposed to go get stuff for you."

"That was old school. I'm the woke, liberated, MeToo boss who buys diapers for his secretary. Wait, that didn't come out right."

She giggled through her tears. Then she got some paper and wrote a list. I rode the elevator down and when I walked out of the building I looked around for Dread. Bernadette had shown me pictures and he'd be easy to spot because he's a tall, skinny guy, tatted up, with wild long black hair. His usual outfit was greasy jeans and a sleeveless tee shirt. All in all, not a banker. I looked, but he was nowhere to be seen. I hailed a taxi and pondered the problem as I rode to the nearest supermarket. I shopped for things I'd never shopped for before. Toddler stuff.

When I got back I was no closer to a solution but Bernadette had cheered up and the kids were rolling around on the carpet with big pillows and stuffed animals. Yes, I'm a hard-boiled private eye. Trouble is my business.

# CHAPTER 11

WHEN IT WAS TIME for our meeting, I was no closer to solving Bernadette's problem. Nails had reluctantly showered and the kids were napping on their air mattress. I called the meeting to order. Well, not really, I just said, "Okay, any new ideas?"

Nails laughed. "Tell them my idea."

"You tell them."

"Okay. I solved which bad guy to pick."

"Wow," said Lucy. "That's great."

"Sure. It's easy. We find a neo-Nazi biker meth dealer corrupt judge who runs a human trafficking gang."

Lucy and Bernadette laughed.

"Why didn't we think of that?" said Bernadette. "So obvious!"

"Genius," said Lucy. "And so easy to find. Should only take a few minutes."

I spoke up.

"While we're looking for the ultimate gangster, Bernadette's got a problem and I think we should solve it."

"What's that?" asked Nails.

"Well, you know she's got this mean ex-boyfriend and that's why she and the kids are staying at the office. He abused her when they were together. Now he knows about this building and is threatening to hurt her if he sees her again."

"Does he know she works for you?" asked Lucy.

"No," said Bernadette, "but he knows I work in this building. He sent me a text, said if he ever found me he was going to mess me up. I have to admit, it's kind of scary."

The room got quiet.

"See," said Lucy, "it's time to switch teams. We lesbians never have trouble with ex-boyfriends."

Bernadette laughed.

"You've got a good point, especially now. But this is my problem, not you guys'. You don't have to get in trouble over my hassles."

"Sure we do," said Nails. "We're a team. Even if you do make up ridiculous shower rules that oppress freedom-loving homeless people. So you don't have choice. We're going to help you and that's that, right boss?"

"Absolutely."

"How'd you hook up with a guy like that?"

"Cocaine. He had it, I wanted it. I thought if I hung with him I'd have an endless supply. Every girl's dream."

"Yeah right," said Lucy. "Why didn't I think of that?."

"At first he was okay, but then he got drunk, drugged up, violent, irrational and mean. When I got sent up it was kind of a relief because he couldn't get to me in prison. Then I cleaned up my act."

"In prison?" Nails exclaimed, "you cleaned up your act in prison?"

"Yeah. I just quit drugs. Cold turkey."

"You've got to be the toughest chick that ever lived. I never heard of anyone doing that."

"Well, it helped that I was in solitary. Got into a fight, punched out my cellmate. I did six weeks in solitary and if that doesn't clean you up, nothing will. When I got out of the hole one of the women took me to a meeting and I've been going ever since."

"No shit?"

"No shit."

"Awesome."

Lucy spoke up.

"Practice!"

"Practice? What do you mean, practice," I asked.

"Dread can be practice! We can kidnap him and practice what we're going to do to the really bad guy."

There was a stunned silence.

"That is awesome," said Nails.

I agreed. Bernadette seemed kind of shocked.

"You all would do that for me?"

"Hey," I said, "this whole venture borders on insanity. Why not compound it? We're in."

"Okay," said Nails, "how do we find him?"

"Easy," I said, "we let him come to us."

And we did. But first we needed some place to put him if we did pull off the kidnapping. Luckily we had Lucy, our chief of construction.

We met later that day and talked about our prison. Yes, private prisons are big in the U.S., why shouldn't we have one? Ours would be easier, as it only needed to hold one person at a time. First Dread, then our criminal mastermind.

"As I see it," I said, "we want to accomplish two things. First, security. We have to keep him locked up and the room has to be soundproofed so he can't yell for help. Any ideas?"

"How about a stand-alone cage in the middle of a room. That way we can soundproof the walls, ceiling and floor," said Lucy.

"That sounds like something out of Hannibal Lecter," said Bernadette.

"Come to think of it, that's probably where I got the idea."

"We'd need a bunk, and a toilet," said Nails. "The toilet would be the hard part."

"It can be done," said Lucy. "If we gut the room, tear out the walls, we can run PVC pipes to the existing toilet. It won't be pretty, but it'll work."

"Do you think we could build it?" I asked.

"Are you guys any good with tools?"

"I'm okay," said Nails. "Not great but I've worked a bit."

"Me too," said Bernadette. "I worked on bikes and stuff."

"I'm useless," I said. "I could change a light bulb in an emergency, but that's about it."

"Okay," said Lucy, "you're in charge of supplies. Now, where are we going to put this prison?"

"I don't want it here," I said, "but down on fourteen we've got two big offices that are vacant. It was a phone center they moved to India. Would one of them do?"

"We'll have to look," she said, "but it sounds good. If it's big, we'll have room for materials and all our tools. Will people complain about the noise?"

"I hadn't thought of that," I said. "Can we work at night?"

"That would be better in a lot of ways," said Lucy. "No noise problems and people won't ask questions when we bring up weird stuff, like bars and soundproofing. Now we get to the big question. Will my money cover it? This will cost a lot."

"We won't use your money for this," I said. "It's not part of your plan. I'll take care of it."

"Can you afford it?" she asked.

Nails laughed. "He can afford to build it out of gold bullion. Didn't you know? We have the richest private eye in the world."

"Seriously?" asked Lucy.

"Seriously," said Nails. "You don't know who owns this building, do you?"

"No."

"He does."

"No shit!"

"No shit."

She looked at me with new eyes.

"Okay," she said, "I can draw up the plans tonight. In fact, we can start the tear down tonight if you want. I've got tools in my truck. You guys like to rip things up?"

"Love it," said Bernadette. "The thought of Dread in a cage is all the incentive I need."

"I'm in," said Nails. "Let's tear down some walls."

# CHAPTER 12

LUCY SPENT THE night measuring and drawing up preliminary plans while we ripped out stuff. I'd never used a crowbar before and it was fun. She figured she'd construct the cage about a foot off the floor to allow for soundproofing under it. She could take out the false ceiling and have room above. Then she'd wall off the windows so the big room would be a square with no windows and just one door. There would be room around the cage for us to pass safely and sit to talk to the prisoner. She knew where to get materials and drew up a preliminary list of things to buy. That was my job.

After four nights of tearing out walls and false ceilings, construction began.

We put up the soundproofing first and it wasn't easy. We got the heavy-duty stuff used in sound studios and did the walls and ceiling, but then we realized we had to do the floor too. How do you soundproof a floor? Lucy checked the Internet and discovered a simple solution—heavy-duty floor soundproofing. We installed that and then laid plywood sheets over it and fastened them down. She had me go buy waterproof garage floor paint and we put a couple of coats on the plywood. Voila! We had a soundproofed room!

But it was time to address the elephant in the room.

How do you build a prison cell without having suppliers figure out what it is? You can't just head down to Jails R Us and pick one out. Lucy realized we could use sections of cast iron fencing and just build a big box. Then she'd lay a plywood floor over the bars on the bottom and bolt it down.

She'd connect the sections of fencing with heavy duty threaded clamps, using allen-head bolts. No sense using something he could unscrew with a coin. Lucy had thought about welding the sections together but felt it'd be better if we could disassemble the cage if we had to.

It wasn't pretty, and took longer than we'd thought, but four weeks later we had a soundproofed room with a square cage in the middle. It had a toilet, and we figured he could sleep on the floor with a pad and blanket. For showers we rigged a hose to a shower head we could hold outside the cage while he showered inside. Again, not pretty, but as foolproof as we could make it.

We thought about a sink, but that was too much plumbing. We figured we could just give him a plastic pan with water and soap.

During a break I said, "We have to talk about phase two. Our plan is to take a confirmed criminal and somehow change his entire personality. I don't think any of us have the tools to do that."

"Boy, tell me," said Bernadette. "Women have been trying to change bad boys for centuries and it never works. I tried and look how that turned out."

"We have to face the fact that we're not psychologists," I said, "and even if we were, I'm not sure they've ever reformed anyone. Look at prisons. People try everything—religion, school, punishment, psychology—and I can't think of anything that really works."

"I'm an engineer," said Lucy, "I hated all that humanities crap. How about you guys?"

"Not a clue," I said. "My dad was basically a crook and I couldn't even change him."

"No shit?" said Nails. "I thought he was a country club rich guy."

"Nope. He was a shyster. He cheated the markets, his friends, the unions, everyone. He was fleeing the country when he got killed."

"Killed?"

"Yeah, blown up by a disgruntled investor. The world's first suicide bomber in a suit. Well, he wasn't wearing a suit at the time, he was in a boat loaded with explosives. Drove it into the side of my dad's yacht."

"Holy crap. I thought you guys lived quiet lives."

"I do. I want no part of that life. To answer the question, I have no skills when it comes to psychiatry or rehabilitation."

"So," said Nails, "So we kidnap a guy, put him in a cage, and then what? Spend years trying to get him to change?"

"Maybe the vigilantes are right," said Bernadette. "Maybe killing bad guys is the only way to go. To bad none of us can do it."

"It's the Hannibal Lecter thing," I said. "They had the top minds in the world working on him and nothing changed. What could we do differently? I think we're stuck."

"Boss," said Bernadette, "I hate to break it to you but that was a movie."

"I knew that," I said, suddenly remembering it was a movie.

"Well," said Lucy. "What about AA? Those people change. They quit drinking."

"Yeah, but they want to. They've hit rock bottom. Our guys don't want to change. Being an awful person works for them."

We couldn't come up with an answer, so we decided to sleep on it. If nothing else, we could keep an evil person out of circulation. That was interesting. Once you remove a criminal mastermind, what happens? Others rush to fill his place. Then, say, he comes back in six months. Do they welcome him with open arms? No way, the new leaders look at him as a threat. Nobody wants to give up power. What would they do? Kill him probably, so we'd be turning the gangsters into vigilantes. I went to sleep with that idea in mind, realizing there were all kinds of possibilities.

# CHAPTER 13

I DIDN'T LIKE the idea of using Bernadette as bait but it was the only thing we could think of. Trying to find Dread alone, in a place we could make a move on him, seemed impossible. On the other hand, if he came after Bernadette, would he bring help? This was personal for him and he was a macho biker. She was a woman he'd dominated. Hopefully he wouldn't bring backup.

We planned it all out. Nails would be the most inconspicuous because nobody looks at homeless people. Also, he was the most physically able to handle Dread if there was a problem. We decided guns were not an option. There was too big a chance of hitting a bystander. Or each other. I had to admit the latter scared me the most. We decided on tasers. One for Bernadette, and one for Nails. We took a solemn vow to try not to tase each other, which would've been embarrassing.

Now we had to get Dread to come to us. If Bernadette asked him to meet he'd be suspicious, maybe bring others. Nails came up with the junkie idea.

"Tell him you need coke. He knew you as an addict and will assume you're back on marching powder. It's believable, and that'll make you seem weaker and more desperate. He'll know he can overpower you."

"That makes sense," said Bernadette.

We went with that.

That night Bernadette typed out a text to Dread.

"Dread. I need help. Please. Just a taste until I can get back on my feet. Please, just this once. I won't hassle you again."

"Does that sound authentic?" I asked the others.

They couldn't think of anything better.

"Okay, send it."

She did. Dread didn't reply right away. A couple hours later he texted.

"I can help. When and where?"

We'd picked the mouth of an alley down the street and she said she'd be there at 11 p.m. He gave her a thumbs up.

"All right," I said. "We want Dread to think she's really harmless. Down and out. Close to being a street person. Lucy, you have to stay here and take care of the kids."

"Well damn," she said. "I want to be in on this too."

We thought about that. Either Lucy or I would have to babysit and we had to decide who would be the most useful on a kidnapping. I could look like a nerdy businessman in a suit. Unthreatening. Lucy, on the other hand, would be tougher than me and could also look unthreatening. We voted. I lost. My first kidnapping and I would be upstairs watching two-year-old twins. I'm a private eye! Shouldn't I be in the heat of the action? Where did I go wrong?

We planned it out, everyone got ready and at 10:30 they headed out.

I went upstairs to babysit.

At 11 p.m., Dread drove slowly up the street in the van. Lucy, looking harmless in a dress, walked the sidewalk across the street and when the van passed under a streetlight she checked to see if he was alone. As far as she could tell, he was. No one beside him, no movement behind him. All systems go.

Dread stopped the van next to the alley and stayed there with the motor running. Lucy walked slowly past across the street. Bernadette came out of the alley looking awful. She'd done a great job of becoming a street person junkie, with tangled hair, dirty sweatshirt, ragged jeans shorts and ratty old sneakers. She had an old backpack over her shoulder. She walked slumped and beaten up the to the passenger side of the van.

"Hi Dread," she said.

"You look like shit," said Dread, ever the smooth talker.

"It's been hard since I got out," she said. "Can you help me?"

"Sure. Hop in the van and I'll hook you up."

"No," she whimpered, "I don't trust you. You'll hurt me."

"No I won't. And I've got a couple lines all laid out for you. Just hop in and everything'll be cool."

"No, Dread, just give me a little baggie. Just a taste and I'll be on my way."

Dread moved across the front seat and opened the passenger door.

"Come on, Bernadette, get in. I'll fix you up. Got lots of coke here and I'm willing to share."

She backed away, looking frightened. "No, you'll hurt me."

"Dread opened the passenger door and got out of the van. Just as he did, Nails staggered out of the alley, a bottle in his left hand, mumbling.

"Spare change Mister?"

"Get out of here! We're busy."

"Come on. Just a quarter, that's all I need. One little quarter."

As he spoke, Nails drew close and held up the bottle, waving it around drunkenly. As he did so, he pulled his right hand around and triggered the taser. Dread stood frozen for a millisecond, then started shaking violently and went down. Bernadette leaped to the van and pulled open the side door. Lucy, who had circled, ran across the street and the three of them threw Dread into the van. Nails jumped on his back, held him down and Bernadette grabbed duct tape out of her backpack. Dread tried to resist, still weak from the taser, but they had him wrapped and gagged in seconds. They slammed the doors shut, Lucy jumped into the driver's seat and pulled sedately away from the curb.

It was done. We were officially kidnappers. An exciting, violent crime and where was I? Up fifteen floors with two sleeping toddlers. Life isn't fair.

Lucy drove to our building and used my key card to get down into the parking garage. She found a place in back by the freight elevator and parked. Nails opened the side door and the dome light shone in the van.

"Well looky looky," said Nails.

On the floor of the van was another roll of duct tape, some plastic ties, a black cloth bag, and pepper spray.

"Looks like we kidnapped a kidnapper," said Lucy.

"Goddamn him," said Bernadette.

They dragged Dread out and got him into the freight elevator and up to the office with our private prison. They took off his belt, all the studs from his piercings, everything in his pockets including a wicked-looking K-Bar knife, and boots. He was left with underwear, jeans and a tee shirt. We put him inside the cage, locked it, and then rolled him over to the bars so we could cut the duct tape.

"Okay," said Nails, "Bernadette, come with me and we'll take the van back. You know where he lives, right?"

"Don't forget to wipe it down," said Lucy.

"Will do."

Nails and Bernadette did a quick cleanup and threw on some better clothes. Then they drove the van back, parked it a block away from Dread's rundown rental house and took a few minutes to wipe it down with rags and bleach. They wore rubber gloves. Then they walked a few blocks away and tossed the bleach, rags and gloves into a dumpster. After that they walked to a bar, stood outside and called a cab.

The deed was done.

## CHAPTER 14

WE ALL SLEPT in the building that night and the next morning went out for breakfast at McDonald's.

"Feels strange eating inside," said Nails.

"Congratulations," I said. "You three did a great job. Bernadette, you can breathe easier now."

"Thank you all," she said. "It'll be so nice to walk around without fear. I realized this morning how much he was bothering me."

I looked around to make sure we were off by ourselves.

"Okay," I said, "first of all, this is a criminal enterprise. We have kidnapped someone, which is federal and carries a long sentence. Awhile ago I watched Tiger King, and what happens to every criminal enterprise? Someone rats out the others when the pressure is on. Does that bother you guys?"

They thought about it awhile, munching on their breakfasts.

"Boss," said Bernadette, "I can't think of any reason for any of us to do that. There's no money involved. No ransom. So what would we gain?"

We thought about that for awhile. Nails came up with the best idea.

"We could go crazy thinking about this stuff," he said. "The truth is, we're in this together and we're all guilty.

Nothing's going to change that, so we better trust each other and do this right."

It seemed like the best solution.

After breakfast we headed back to the building. We wanted to be there when Dread woke up. We walked into his prison room and it was pitch black because we'd boarded up all the windows and covered them with soundproofing. We switched on the lights and knew he had no idea if it was day or night. The light woke him up.

"What the fuck!!!! What the hell is this?"

We sat in chairs like spectators as he stood up. He started shaking the bars and yelling. He saw Bernadette first.

"You bitch!" he yelled, "what the fuck is this? I'll kill you, you fucking junkie. I'll cut you into little pieces!"

I had the feeling rehabilitation was going to be a long, long process. Bernadette, on the other hand, seemed quite pleased with the situation. She was laughing and giving him the finger.

"Oh Dread, shut the fuck up. No one's going to hear you and if you don't calm down we'll just leave for a few hours until you do."

"Who wants coffee?" said Lucy. Everyone said yes, except Dread who was still cursing. Lucy went out to get some and Nails, Bernadette and I just sat and watched Dread. He cursed, paced, and cursed some more.

"I'll kill all you fuckers," he promised. "You're going down! When my boys find out, you are dead. Dead."

We let him rave on. We'd agreed to just let him rant until he got tired. Lucy came back with the coffee and we sat, drinking and watching Dread. It only made him madder. He yelled and paced the cage and shook the bars but we'd tested them and they didn't move. He punched the air, and screamed. We just sat and watched.

Finally he ran out of steam.

"What the fuck is this?" he said, in a calmer tone.

I answered.

"Well, you threatened our friend Bernadette and we couldn't let that happen. We don't want her hurt."

"Okay, I won't hurt her. Let me out of here."

I laughed.

"Seriously? You were going to kidnap her! No, you're going to be in that cage a long time."

"You can't do that. It's not legal."

"I'm afraid legal went out the window when you threatened Bernadette. Think of this as a private matter."

"Where are we?"

"We can't tell you that."

"There must be people around somewhere. I'll make noise. They'll hear."

"Nope. This room is soundproofed. There could be people next door and they won't hear a thing. Go ahead, scream all you want."

"Who are you people?"

"We're Bernadette's friends. You mess with her, you deal with us."

"Color me scared. Two old guys and two bitches? Soon as I get out you're all dead."

"You're not getting out."

"My boys will look for me. They'll find me."

"I doubt it. Nobody followed us, nobody knows where we are."

"What about food? You got to feed me."

"Bernadette is in charge of food. If you want to eat or drink you'll have to ask her. I'd advise you to ask her nicely."

"Fuck that. I'm not asking that bitch for anything."

"Okay. It's your choice. There are video cameras in here so just let her know when you want something to eat or drink. Nicely. Let her know nicely. We have to go now so make yourself at home. See you in a few hours."

We got up and walked out.

"You actually think we can change this guy?" Lucy asked when we got out into the hall.

"I doubt it," I said. "I have no idea how to do that. Do you?"

"No."

"Nails? Any ideas?"

"None," said Nails. "I've had people trying to change me for the last fifteen years and none of it worked. They wanted me to clean up, get a job, you even tried to get me off the streets and into an apartment. No one could change me."

"So you've got no ideas?"

"None. And if you try religion I'm out of here. Those religious people kept trying to get me and I want no part of that."

"I don't think any of us are religious," said Bernadette. "You know, when you think of it he's our prisoner and we're his. We have to stay and watch him."

"Not really," said Lucy. "We've got cameras on him and we can watch from our computers or phones. He's not going anywhere."

"Still," I said, "we should keep a close watch. He might find something we haven't thought of."

"What if he gets sick?" asked Lucy.

That stopped us. We hadn't thought of it. We decided we'd figure that out if it happened. We knew we couldn't let him die but we couldn't let him see a doctor either. Oh well, every plan has its flaws.

For awhile we sat in my office and watched Dread on video. We heard him mumbling to himself as he paced his cell. In time he lay down on the pad and slept some more. We relaxed in my office and talked while the toddlers played.

"Don't you get any business?" Lucy asked. "If someone

were to walk in they'd think they'd found a daycare center, not a detective agency."

"He doesn't exactly hustle business," said Bernadette. "If someone does come, Willie down at the desk will warn us and you can all head for the conference room. I'll pretend to be a secretary."

"Pretend?" I said. "I hired you. You are my secretary."

"Come on, boss," she said, "you know I could do this job in about an hour. The rest of the time I pretend. I think I answered the last phone call three days ago, and that was some guy who wanted you to play golf."

"You play golf?" asked Nails.

"I used to," I said. "Then I realized I wasn't going to get any better and lost interest. I haven't played in months."

"You any good?"

"I used to be. I was on the college team. Now, probably not."

The conversation dwindled for awhile.

"You know," said Lucy, "I've never even seen a real jail."

"Really?" said Nails, "None of your family's ever been in prison?"

"Nope. Mom and Dad lived a normal life and my big brothers didn't get into trouble."

"How many brothers and sisters did you have?"

"One sister, two brothers."

"Where'd you grow up?"

"In Idaho. We lived in Boise for awhile and then moved up to Sandpoint. I loved it there. Skiing, hiking, fishing, all that outdoor stuff."

"Sandpoint is kind of redneck isn't it? Didn't they have some neo-Nazis up there?"

"There were about six of them but you'd have thought there was an army. They got a lot of press. Mostly it was just a small mountain town and I miss the mountains."

"Why don't you live there?"

"Oh I came to Seattle for college, got hung up on work here, started my company and stayed.

"You have a girlfriend?"

"I did, but we split up. No great battles or anything, we just drifted apart."

"That happens," said Nails. "What about your sister and brothers?"

"They're fine and we stay in touch. A couple of years ago I built my brother's house."

"No kidding."

"Yeah, he's got a wife and kids and they live over on Bainbridge Island. They bought a lot and we designed a house together. I built it."

"Alone?"

"No, I've got friends in construction and I hired them. The house came out nice, my brother and his wife were happy."

Just then, we noticed Dread waking up.

"Anyone there?" he called.

I went over to the microphone on my desk.

"Yeah, we're here."

"I want food. You can't starve me in here. And I need water too."

"That would be Bernadette's job. She is the food boss. We'll come in."

We walked over to the prison office and went in.

"I need food and water."

"Okay," I said. "Ask Bernadette."

"Fuck that. I ain't asking that bitch for nothin'. You got to feed me."

"Why? You think we're under the Geneva Convention? We don't have to do a damn thing."

"You can't let me starve."

"Why not? You were going to do horrible things to her. Wouldn't bother me a bit."

"Fuck it. I'm not askin' her nothin.'"

"Okay. Actually, I'm ready for lunch now, how about you guys?"

They agreed and I went down to the Thai place and got some pad Thai, Penang gai and pad see ew. I brought it up and we sat around the table outside his cell eating lunch.

"You fuckers," he yelled. "You got to feed me!"

"You hear anything, Bernadette?" asked Lucy.

"Nope, just background noise." she answered.

"Goddamn it Bernadette I need food."

"Boy," said Nails, "that didn't sound nice at all. He didn't even say *please*.

Dread punched the air. He cursed. Then he came to the bars and said through gritted teeth, "Bernadette, can I have some food? Please?"

He nearly strangled getting the last word out.

Bernadette looked up. "Why sure, Dread, no problem. I'll be right back."

She went down to the Seven Eleven and got a couple microwave hot dogs, nuts, yogurt and bottled water. She brought it into the room and said, "I'm not giving it to him."

Nails said, "I'll do it" and took the bag over to the cell.

"Stand back," he said to Dread. "Other side of the cell."

Dread did and he emptied the bag on the floor. Dread grabbed a water bottle and took a long pull. Then he looked at the food. He was about to say something but he was too hungry and he wolfed it down.

"How come I get this crap and you guys get good food?"

"Because," said Nails, "you're an asshole and we're nice people. Also, you're in prison. We're trying to give you the authentic experience."

"You fuckers. How long you going to keep me here?" he asked.

"We haven't figured that out," I said. "We can't let you go because you're a threat to all of us now. So it could be a long time."

"That's stupid. You're going to keep me locked up for what, years?"

"Like I say, we haven't figured that out," I said. "We can't let you out as long as you're a danger to us and I can't see that changing in my lifetime. You got any ideas?"

"You'll never change me. Somehow, I'm going to get out of here and I'm coming for all of you. Bank on that."

"As I said, it could be a long time."

We finished our lunch, Nails made Dread pick up the wrappings and plastic bottle and toss them outside the cell. We gathered them up and left.

That night I slept in the office with Bernadette and the kids next door. I felt protective. Nails went out roaming the streets and Lucy went back to her house to work on the houseboat plans for our next president.

## CHAPTER 15

WE ATE BREAKFAST outside the cell, with Dread now asking Bernadette nicely for the food but always through gritted teeth. Then I had them gather around to tell them my new idea.

"First of all, I think Dread is a really stupid name. What's your real name?"

"Fuck you," said Dread.

"Odd name," I replied. "Were your parents on drugs at the time? And here's our new baby, Fuck You. Fuck you, here's your brother, Cocksucker."

The others laughed.

"I can tell you his name," said Bernadette, "it's here in his wallet. Eugene. Eugene Walker. I bet people called him Gene."

"Kind of a sissy name," said Nails. "No wonder he switched to Dread. What about it, Dread? You get beat up in high school? You the class wimp?"

"Fuck you. Nobody beat me up. I was big."

"Probably got held back a grade or two, right?"

"No way. And nobody fucked with me."

"Oh boy," said Nails. "Gene here was a tough guy in high school. You play football?"

"Sports are stupid."

"Got it. You were with the guys out smoking and drinking behind the stadium. Gangsters, right?"

"Tough enough. People didn't fuck with us."

"Got the picture. Lousy student, outcast, bad boy, probably terrorized the little kids, right?"

"None of your fucking business old man. Leave me alone."

"Okay, you got it." said Nails, and he turned back to us.

"Not the world's greatest conversationalist, is he?" I said.

We nodded.

His withdrawals started the next day. He'd been using all kinds of drugs and liquor and Bernadette warned us about what he'd be going through. It wasn't pretty. We told him to throw up in the toilet, but sometimes he didn't make it. We just hosed him off but realized the water was running off onto the floor and might screw up the soundproofing underneath. This was a problem and would be with our shower plan too. Lucy solved it by rigging a big PVC gutter around the outside of the cage and caulking it. She then piped that to the toilet drain. Not pretty, but it worked.

"Can he break off some of that pipe and use it as a weapon?" I asked.

"Have you ever tried to break PVC?"

"No."

"Well no one's that strong. It'll be fine."

For a week he went through it all. Sweats, shakes, writhing in pain, hallucinations, crying, begging for drugs and liquor, screaming at us, the works. We didn't comfort him, but we did keep a close watch.

We tried to keep him hydrated, and gave him ice and cold towels, but Bernadette told us there wasn't much else we could do. She'd gone through it in worse conditions in solitary confinement, so I think she kind of enjoyed watching him struggle.

Finally he emerged, weak, a few pounds lighter, desperate for water, and able to keep down a little bit of food. Needless to say, he wasn't his old belligerent self, but he was still angry.

"You fuckers," he whispered. "I will get you for this. I swear I will get you."

"Hey," I said, "it's a lot cheaper than the Betty Ford clinic and we guarantee results. Look at the bright side, we don't bother with meetings and councilors. We just get you clean and keep you clean whether you want to be or not. Welcome back to reality."

"I will get you," he promised.

He just wasn't a happy-go-lucky guy.

# CHAPTER 16

A COUPLE DAYS later we sat in Dread's room. We realized there was no reason to keep anything secret from him, because if he ever got out, he could put us all in prison anyway.

"So, everybody," I said, "we have a problem. We've solved Bernadette's hassle with Dread by kidnapping him. He can't hurt her now. But the only way we can ever let him go is by knowing he won't hurt her ever again. And, we have to know he won't rat us out for kidnapping.

"Ideally, we'd take this nasty bastard and turn him into an upstanding citizen but none of us have the tools to do that. Last night I realized there's only one person who can solve this."

"Who?" they asked.

"Him. He's got to figure out a way to convince us he'll never try to harm any one of us."

"Shit," said Nails, "he'll just fake it. Say he's sorry, he'll never be bad again."

"I know. And we know that. So he's got to convince the four of us he's changed."

"I'm not changing a fucking thing," said Dread.

"If he doesn't, we only have one option," said Nails.

"What's that?"

"We have to kill him. It's the only way we'll really know we're safe."

For some reason, Dread stayed quiet. Apparently he hadn't thought of that possibility.

Lucy spoke up.

"How long can we go before we have to decide?"

"I'm good for awhile," I said, "how about you guys?"

"Yeah," said Bernadette. "I kind of like watching him in a cage. I'm good for a long time after what he did to me."

"So, Dread," I said. "You can take your time, but at some point you've got to figure out a way to convince us it's safe to let you out. Personally, I have no idea how you're ever going to do that so we're in it for the long haul."

"Bernadette will get you food and water as long as you ask nicely and we'll keep watch."

"You fuckers are crazy," said Dread.

"Have you ever done a sentence without the word 'fuck' in it? I think you're going for some kind of record."

"Fuck you."

"Yes! You're on a roll!"

We sat around and talked about other things for awhile and then we left Dread sitting on his pad, mumbling to himself. Angry. Mean. Rehabilitation? Not a chance in hell.

We fell into a routine. Lucy worked hours on the houseboat plans. Bernadette handled the meals. I gave Dread a shower every day. I gave him the option of taking off his clothes or spending the rest of the day in wet ones. He refused to take off his clothes for a couple of days, then changed his mind.

I'd stand outside the cage and spray the water in while he soaped up and got clean. Then I'd give him a towel and a clean jumpsuit. I wasn't enthused about seeing him naked, but we couldn't think of any other way. For a tough guy, he didn't have a lot of scars or bullet holes. I remarked on that and he gave us his usual. "Fuck you." The guy was a one-trick pony.

We all spent random times in the cell room.

Bernadette liked to meditate. She'd begun in solitary and kept it up, so every day she'd bring a cushion in and sit for two hours. At first he would yell at her to try to interrupt, but she just ignored it and eventually he quit. One time he tried to piss on her through the bars but he was too far away. She mopped up the piss and cut out a day's food in return. He didn't do it again.

Sometimes Bernadette would just stare at him. He'd try to talk but she didn't feel like talking to him so she didn't. I think she was just trying to figure out how she could've been under his spell for so long. Of course, the cocaine was the major attraction, but she could've gotten it somewhere else. How could this guy have abused her so long? She just sat and stared.

Nails? He went back to the streets, but sometimes he cleaned up and spent time with us. One day we helped him hang a heavy bag in the prison room and sometimes would come in for a workout. He'd warm up, skipping rope, and then he'd go for awhile on the heavy bag. Dread seemed to think it was weird, an old guy working out like that.

When Lucy visited, she'd lie on the floor outside the cage and work on the plans for the houseboat, changing little things, trying to make them better. She wore her usual jeans, sweatshirt and work boots and Dread, a deep thinker, only took a couple of weeks to realize she was gay. As soon as he did, the dike remarks came and Lucy just laughed.

"Come on, Dread," she said, "I spend my life in construction sites. You got to do better than that. What are you? A pussy?"

He tried to get worse, but she just laughed and soon he ran out of ideas. Every day he'd try to get to her and every day she'd laugh and tell him to work on his material. In time he gave up.

Me, I'd go in and read. Sometimes I'd read aloud and Dread would ignore me. He'd lie down on his pad and pretend to be asleep, but I knew it broke the monotony for him. We couldn't let him out to exercise, but Nails pointed out he could chin himself on the bars up above and do push-ups and sit-ups, and jog in place.

At first he went through a lot of anger, resentment, yelling, pacing, beating the bars, shaking them, and then he went through periods of withdrawal. He'd sit on his pad, rocking, or just silently sitting. Not talking. He was trying to cope and he had no idea how. Sometimes, alone, when he thought no one was watching, he cried.

About three weeks in, he started yelling again.

"I want TV," he cried. "I'm going crazy in here. You people are worse than I am."

We thought about that. We weren't here to torture him, and life in a small cell was a form of torture. Were we that kind of people?

"Movies," I said. "We can control the input, maybe we can affect the outcome. What if we give him a steady diet of uplifting movies? Positive things."

"We could also pipe in lectures off the Internet. Give him a diet of history and philosophy, wake him up to the great ideas of the world."

"Music," said Bernadette. "He plays bass so he has to like music. We could play music videos."

"Interesting," I said. "Did you ever read about the experiment where they put a rat in a cage with two tubes? One had food and one had cocaine? After awhile the rat would just go to the cocaine tube. Then he'd starve to death."

"Yeah," said Nails. "I heard about that."

"It's famous, but it's wrong. They did another

experiment years later where they did the same thing but they put toys and other rats in the cage. The rats didn't bother with the cocaine. Apparently, you turn to drugs when you're bored and not a part of society."

"Boy, if there's one person who's bored and not a part of society, it's Dread," said Bernadette. "If it weren't for the band, he didn't have a friend in town. He spent his days on the couch, bored out of his skull. Then he'd do drugs and liquor and get violent."

"Okay," said Nails. "We don't want him going psycho on us. Let's give him some TV and stuff.

So we let Dread watch movies. *Groundhog Day, Mr. Smith Goes to Washington, Good Will Hunting, The Shawshank Redemption,* even *The Sound of Music.* Once you Google "uplifting movies" you have a lot to choose from. We also found lectures and interviews about history, social studies, psychology, music, art, philosophy and piped those in too.

One day Lucy went in and sat for awhile.

"What's it like, being a dyke," he asked.

"I prefer the term *bull dyke.*"

"Yeah, right. But you'll never be a real man."

"Nope. I know that. I just have to do the best I can with what I've got."

"You got a dyke girlfriend?"

"Not now. I had a few over the years."

"Every want to beat the crap out of them?"

"Sure, lots of times, but I never did."

"Why," he sneered, "it's not moral?"

"No. Because it's stupid. Beating up people is stupid."

"You know I beat up Bernadette."

"I know."

"You calling me stupid?"

"Hell yes. You're a fucking idiot."

"Okay, now we're talking!"

"We sure are. You're stupid and you're mean. That's why people don't like you."

"I got friends."

"Bullshit."

"I do. And they're going to find you sick bastards and take you out."

"Whoo, I'm scared."

"You should be."

"First of all, your friends are too stupid to find us, and second, they're not looking. I'd say it took them about a day to forget you ever existed."

"Bullshit. My bros are out there lookin.'"

"Yeah. Sure they are. They're out there lookin' to score drugs and pussy. You're not even on the list."

"No way. We're a band. We stick together. They're lookin.'"

"Want to bet on it? Let's go on their Twitter page and see if they got a new bass player yet."

"I don't trust you. You'll put up some bogus post just to fuck with me."

"Okay. But think about it. How long would you look if your drummer went missing? I'm guessing a day or two because hey, a stoner goes missing, what's new? And drummers are a dime a dozen."

"You're trying to mess with me."

"No, I'm trying to get you to deal with the truth."

Lucy believed what she was saying. No way a couple of druggie musicians would spend time looking for this loser. Was there?

"How'd you get so mean?" she asked.

"Maybe I was born mean. Maybe I like biker bars and thrash rock and fights and slapping the shit out of people who bother me."

"Could be. I haven't a clue how people like you get that way."

"So why are you trying to mess with my head? Tryin' to fix me?"

"I'm not. I couldn't do it if I tried. I'm just happy you're in there where you can't hurt people. I figure it's a public service."

"You can't keep me here forever."

"Well, I'm younger than you, so I could keep you here till you got really old. Then you wouldn't be a threat. Once you're feeble, in a wheelchair, I'd be happy to let you go."

"Bullshit. I'll outlast you all."

"Maybe. But we've still got a life. We can go out and work, party, hang out, and you're stuck in that cell. Who do you thinks going to last the longest?"

"Fuck you."

"That's kind of your go-to phrase isn't it?"

"Fuck you."

"I don't think so. You're playing for the wrong team."

"If I was out of here I'd fuck you up."

"Maybe, or maybe I'd bust you with a roofing hammer. We'll never know, 'cause you're not getting out. I got to go now. I got a date with a hot chick. Remember when you could do that?"

"I'll kill you, you fucking dyke."

Lucy laughed as she walked out the door.

## CHAPTER 17

ONE DAY NAILS walked in wearing his homeless clothes, coming off a binge. I'd given him keys to the back door of the building and the freight elevator so he wouldn't have to get past Willie in the lobby. He could come and go as he pleased.

He was still half drunk, his hair and beard were matted, he was mumbling incoherently. He stripped off his filthy old homeless coat and sweaters, got down to pants and a ratty old tee shirt. Dread watched as he staggered around a bit, shadow boxing, and then he clumsily wrapped his hands and went to work on the heavy bag. The punches barely landed. He almost fell down trying to dance around. Dread laughed. Nails looked up and laughed with him.

"What's the matter?" he said. "You never seen a drunk work out before?"

"No," said Dread, "but it is funny. What the hell are you trying to do?"

"Sweat out some booze. This might take awhile."

He punched the bag some more, barely making a dent, mumbling. Then he grabbed his filthy clothes and left the room.

He took the elevator up to the penthouse and walked through the guest room and into the bathroom. He took a long, long shower and dried off. Then he flopped on the floor in a bathrobe and slept fourteen hours straight.

He woke up with a dry mouth and pounding headache. He rushed to the bathroom and threw up, then he showered again and put on a sweat suit.

In the kitchen he brewed coffee and drank it while forcing down a couple pieces of dry toast. He felt a tiny bit better. Later he walked back down to the prison room.

He jumped rope. Slowly. Trying to work up a sweat, get more of the liquor out of him.

Then as Dread watched, he moved to the heavy bag and started in. It was more impressive, the punches starting out slowly but later landing with a little authority. He lasted as long as he could, then flopped down on a chair to drink water and pant from the exertion.

"You used to fight?" said Dread.

"Yeah."

"Bet I could whip your ass."

"Probably. You're twenty years younger."

"Why don't you open up this cage and we'll see."

"I don't fight thug wannabes. I fight real fighters."

"You're scared."

"Nope. I just got my pride."

"I been in fights."

"Yeah, right. Bar fights. Drunks throwing roundhouses."

"I been in big fights. Biker fights. Clubs and brass knuckles, beer bottles, pool cues. Not that sissy shit with gloves."

"Okay. You're younger and tougher. So what? You're in there and I'm out here."

"One time. Just let me out one time and we'll see who's tough."

"Nope. I proved how tough I am, I don't have to do it again."

"What'd you fight? Golden gloves? Amateur shit?"

"Yeah. I did that."

"That's it?"

"No. I turned pro. Fought about ten years."

"You one of those guys they bring in to tune up the champions? One of those tin cans?"

"Oh, you know the lingo. I'm impressed. Maybe when you get out you can Google me, see if I was good or not. It don't matter now."

"I'll say. Looks like you're on the streets now, so you couldn't have been that good. You fight the other bums now?"

"Nope. I just stay quiet. My fighting days are over."

"Looks like your money days are over too. What's it like to be a bum?"

"Not that great, but nobody tells me what to do or where to go."

"What do you do for money, beg?"

"I do that. I clean windshields. But mostly I just roam around. It beats working."

"Seriously? No bed, no showers, sleeping in doorways? You call that a good life?"

"Naw, it's a shitty life. But it's all mine. I can deal with it."

"Yeah, but you're getting old fast. Soon you won't be able to protect yourself. I see those bums out there. People give them all kinds of shit."

"That's why we stay dirty. People don't want to get near us. It's protection."

"It's a stupid fucking life if you ask me."

"Well, it beats being in a cell. You liking it in there?"

"I'll get out some day. And when I do, you guys are dead. All of you."

"Keep saying that. I'll pretend it's you when I'm hitting the bag."

"You're past it old man. No sense trying to get it back. You're just a bum."

"Right you are. I'm just a bum. But hitting the bag brings back memories. I liked training. Maybe I liked it more that fighting. Who knows."

"Hey, can you get me some good movies? This feel good shit is driving me crazy. Get me something with action!"

"Not going to happen. Your action days are over."

Dread got up and started throwing punches in his cell.

"Fuck that. I'll get out of here and when I do, I'll show you action."

"Those the punches you threw in bars? Those the ones made you a tough guy?"

"Tough enough. I laid a few guys out."

"Fuck me. They must've been real stiffs. A boxer would take you down in about ten seconds."

"Not if I hit them first."

"You couldn't hit a fighter with those punches. I could duck them and I'm fifty. I can't believe you called me a tin can."

"Let me out old man, we'll see who beats who."

"Nah, I'd kill you. You better stick to women. Takes a real man to beat up a woman."

"Fuck you. She deserved it."

"Dream on. You're just a scumbag lowlife and you're not going to change. Ever. Get used to that cell, 'cause it's gonna be yours for a long time."

"Not a chance. I'll get out. Mark my words. And I'll be coming for you."

"Keep practicing those punches. I can't wait to step inside them and kick your ass."

Nails went back to the bag, and the thumping of his fists was disquieting.

# CHAPTER 18

BERNADETTE SPENT MOST of her time in my office with her kids and soon it wasn't an office any more. I knew she could go back to her apartment now, she was safe, but it became obvious she liked the office better. She had us for support and also it was a huge load off her mind knowing she had three other people helping with the kids. Surprisingly, Nails was the best. The kids loved him, especially when he showered, and he loved them. Instinctively he knew when to play around and when to back off. So he became Uncle Nails and the kids always brightened up when he came in the room.

We basically converted her conference room into a one-room apartment. We brought up a bed for Bernadette. We also brought up cribs for the kids but they screamed when we tried to put them in. They loved sleeping on the floor, and we realized it was safer. It's hard to fall out of a floor. So we went back to the air mattresses and they were happy campers.

The conference room had a bathroom and sink and soon it also had a microwave, a toaster oven, a hot plate, a blender and a refrigerator. After years of drug life and an abusive boyfriend, Bernadette now had a family. Okay, it was a strange family, but it was better than a bunch of bikers.

One day we drove over to her apartment, gathered up her belongings and moved out. It was an awful place, and she was happy to see the last of it.

# CHAPTER 19

HAVE YOU EVER had a time when you kidnapped someone, put him in a cage in an office downstairs, then came to work one morning and found a couple of police detectives waiting for you? I can tell you, it's a heart stopper. I walked in and saw these two gentlemen. One of them flashed a badge and I almost panicked. Surprisingly, I managed to speak.

"Good morning officers, what can I do for you?"

The shorter of the two, a black man who looked like he spent a lot of time in the gym, said, "Sorry to bother you sir, but we're investigating a crime."

"Okay, what do I have to do with it?"

"We didn't come to talk to you, sir, we'd like a few words with your secretary, Bernadette Malone."

"Okay, but can I ask you what it's about? How is Bernadette involved in a crime?"

"Maybe we can talk to her first. Is she here?"

"She should be in the next room. Let me get her for you."

I walked over to the conference room, knocked, and Bernadette opened the door. Softly I said, "The police are here. Stay calm. They want to talk to you."

"No problem, boss, I've talked to a lot of cops in my time. Let's see what they want."

She came out and said, "Hi, I'm Bernadette. What's this all about?"

"I'm detective Tan," said the short guy, and this is detective Ormood. "We're investigating a disappearance."

"Oh no. A kid?"

"No, it's an adult and we think you knew him."

"Could be. Who was it?"

"Mr. Gene Walker, goes by the name of Dread."

"Oh I know him all right. You say he disappeared?"

"Yes. How did you know this man?"

"Well, he used to be my boyfriend until he started beating me up. That's why me and the kids are hiding in this office. He's been stalking me and threatening so I asked Monte if I could stay here for awhile."

"He's an abuser?"

"Yeah, you can check your records. I reported him. I been afraid to go out for the last two months 'cause I know he's looking for me."

"Can you describe him?"

"Sure. About 6'4", skinny as a rail but strong, lots of tattoos, long, greasy black hair, hooked nose, and mean as a snake. You think something bad happened to him?"

"It's possible ma'am."

"Well whoop de doo. You think it was bikers? He hangs out with bikers. And musicians. If it was me, I'd put my money on the bikers."

"We don't know who did what. As a matter of fact it was a couple of band guys who called it in. Can't be much of a band. We interviewed them and they looked more like thugs than musicians."

"Yeah, I know those guys too."

"Right," said Officer Tan, "do you know anyone who'd want to cause him harm?"

"Oh hell yes. About half the druggies in this city hate

his guts. Same with his old girlfriends. You won't be short of suspects."

"You haven't heard from anyone have you? No ransom demands."

Bernadette laughed long and loud. "Ransom? Me? Shit, I'd pay them to keep him. He hurt me and I've got the hospital records to prove it. You think it was a kidnapping and not a hit? If someone killed the bastard I could walk the streets again without looking over my shoulder."

"We don't have a theory. Anything's possible. Anything else you can think of to help us?"

"No, but my money's on a rival biker gang or someone he cheated on a drug deal. Dread was a low life son of a bitch."

"Wow, you really hated the guy. You didn't pay someone to take him out did you?"

"Officer, I got two kids and I get secretary money. I might be able to scrape together fifteen bucks on a good day. I bet hit men charge a lot more than that."

"Okay ma'am, and we're sorry for what he did to you. If we find him and he causes you any trouble, you can call me and Jim here. My first name is Richard. We'll come any time, day or night, and we'll believe you."

"You'd take my word against his?"

"Yours and most of the other people we've interviewed. What you said meshes with what everyone else says. To tell you the truth, I'm not highly motivated to find this guy."

"I appreciate that."

"But we have to do our job."

He turned to me.

"Did you know Dread?"

"No. Never met the man, but he sounds dangerous. Bernadette's told me stories."

"Okay. Thank you both for your help. We'll definitely let you know if the case breaks."

We said, "Thank you," and the officers left.

"I don't think we should tell Dread the police are on the case," I said.

"For sure," she said. "Don't encourage the bastard."

# CHAPTER 20

WITH DREAD IN a cage, Bernadette felt it was safe to go out and she started making trips to the Korean grocery for kid stuff—diapers, food, all those things. She didn't know it, but the guys in Dread's band were really pissed off. Apparently, Dread had been the lead singer/song writer. Who knew? At the gigs she got high, danced all night and didn't pay much attention to the band. All she knew was they were loud, Dread screamed unintelligible lyrics and they had a good beat. Apparently, Dread was more important to them than she thought.

Also, they'd known he'd planned to meet Bernadette. After that, nothing. He was gone. One day his band guys were cruising downtown, killing time.

Dex, the lead guitarist, saw her first. Dex was the shorter of the two, with lank blond hair, lots of piercings and tats, and was wearing jeans and a Kid Rock tee shirt. Earl was a skinhead, muscular with roundness to him. Round head, round body, and he was wearing ripped jeans and a wife-beater shirt to show off his tattoos of knives, skulls, stormtrooper insignia, and other threats. Surprisingly, both were moderately good musicians but their heavy metal heritage was way behind the times and even with Dread the band had been struggling. Without him, the bookings had dried up and they were desperate.

"That's her!" yelled Dex, almost causing Earl to spill hot coffee.

"Fuck man, you almost got me burned!"

"Sorry, bro, but that was Bernadette. She just walked into that 7-Eleven."

"So what?"

"Dread was going to pick her up when he disappeared."

"Pick her up my ass. He was going to teach her a lesson."

"Yeah, but he never came back. She might know something."

"Okay, what do we do?"

"We can't cause a scene on the street, too many people."

"She has to come back out that door, and we can follow her."

"Okay, let's do it."

"I'm going to get out and follow on foot." said Dex. "You stay with the van and keep your phone on speaker. I'll tell you which way to go."

It was a perfect plan, except Bernadette never came back out. She'd seen the van and recognized it. The 7-Eleven was the closest store and she'd walked in. Luckily there was a woman behind the counter.

"I need help," said Bernadette. "I'm running from my boyfriend. I don't want to get beat up any more. Can you get me out the back door?"

The woman looked up. "I can do better than that, sister. I can get you out the back door and call the cops."

"No, no cops. I filed a report and they didn't do a damn thing. I'm leaving town, going a long way from here. If he comes in, just delay him if you can but don't push it. He's mean."

"Okay sister, I got your back. Follow me."

The woman got her out the back door and Bernadette took off running down the alley. Dex waited across from the 7-Eleven but Bernadette didn't come out.

"Earl," he said into his phone, "She's been in there a long time. I'm going in."

"She'll recognize you."

"I know, but what if she slipped out another door?"

"Give it another couple of minutes. We don't want to blow this."

"Okay."

They waited.

"I'm going in."

"Okay bro, let me know."

Dex walked in the store and looked up and down the aisles. No Bernadette, just the woman behind the counter and a guy stocking bottled water. Dex went up to the counter.

"Did you see a woman come in here? Black hair, jeans, Levis jacket?"

"People come in all day, I don't pay attention."

"Come on. You haven't had a customer in ten minutes."

"Okay. I saw her. You the guy who beats up women?"

"What the hell?"

"She told me all about you. Said you beat her up, so I let her out the back door. She's long gone."

Dex started to argue but thought better of it.

"Let me out the back door. Now!"

"No."

"Damn it, bitch, let me out before I come over that counter and make you."

She pointed behind her.

"You see that camera? This is all recorded. I bet the cops know you. I've also got you on a 911 call."

She pulled her phone from behind the cash register.

"The 911 operator is right here, want to talk to her?"

"Fuck you," yelled Dex, and turned and rushed out.

The boy stocking the shelves came over.

"That was good thinking, calling 911."

"I didn't call 911. Want to talk to my boyfriend?"

She held up the phone.

The kid laughed.

"You think I stalled the guy long enough?"

"Oh hell yes. That woman is safe."

I WAS IN THE OFFICE watching the kids when Bernadette got back. I could tell she was flustered.

"What's wrong?"

"Dex and Earl spotted me."

"I'm guessing those are the guys from the band?"

"Yeah. Dex plays lead guitar, Earl is on drums. Dex isn't a really bad guy, but Earl is nasty. I think he's kind of a Nazi-type and he's strong and mean."

"Well damn. That's not good news. I thought they'd quit looking long ago."

"Me too," she said.

"Did they follow you here?"

"No, I ditched them. You know that 7-Eleven over on Union?"

"Yeah."

"If you go in there and see a woman behind the counter with black hair, bangs, looks about forty, can you slip her fifty bucks? She got me out the back way and promised to stall them."

"I'll give her more than that. Got to admire people who step up for a stranger. So those guys saw you four blocks from here. You think they can figure out where you are?"

"I doubt it. I didn't meet you until after prison so they never heard of you. But they're out there."

"You'll have to be careful. From now on you and Nails can take one of my cars and shop out of the city. You can use the Toyota. It's brown and nondescript with dark tinted windows. I bought it so I could tail suspects without them noticing."

"Did you ever tail a suspect?"

"Well, no. But I'm ready if I ever have to."

"I can't believe I work for a private eye who's never tailed anyone."

"It's only been four years. My time will come. The good news is you can use the car."

"Okay Boss, and thank you. I've got enough stuff now so I think I'll lie low for a few days."

"Okay. Let's play it safe from now on. I'm going to go see how our prisoner is doing."

Bernadette took her boys back to the conference room. I went down to our private prison. I opened the door and Dread was standing in his cell, naked. Lucy was sitting in a chair ten feet away laughing.

"Dread," she said, giggling, "I've seen guys before. You think a little weenie wagging is going to upset me?"

I stood in the doorway and watched.

"Listen, bitch, when I get out of her I'm going to find you and screw your ass. I'm going to show you what real fucking is like."

"Oh hell, Dread, I've been with men. I just never liked it. Put your clothes back on and grow up."

Dread realized his attempt to shock her wasn't working. He lay down on his mat, still naked, staring at the ceiling. I walked in the room, said hi to Lucy and walked over to the cage.

"Hi Dread. You want to put your clothes back on?"

"Fuck you," he said, bitterly.

I walked over and turned the thermostat down to fifty.

"Lucy, you might want to go back now, it's going to get cold."

"Okay," she said. "But I wouldn't mind staying around watching Dread's weenie get smaller and smaller. Hard to be macho man with that going on."

"Up to you."

I sat beside her in one of the office chairs and watched as the temperature dropped. Dread resisted for awhile, then reluctantly grabbed his coveralls and put them on. I turned the thermostat back up and sat back down with Lucy. We talked in conversational tones but we were close enough that Dread could hear.

"You know," said Lucy, "there is a possibility that Dread might never change. You have to admire his ability to stick to his mean, disgusting personality."

"I know," I said. "I thought he'd be thinking this through by now."

"We're looking at a long-term project."

"It's okay with me."

Dread spoke up.

"You can't keep me here forever. You're going to break before I will. You're just a bunch of pussies."

"That could be," I said. "But we're pussies who can go out to a restaurant, get a good meal, go to concerts, wander the city, be with loved ones. I bet you miss all that."

"Fuck you. You guys are insane. You can't keep me locked up like this. Even in prison you get to go out and exercise."

"I know. It's just brutal and wrong." I said. "But then again, so is trying to kidnap Bernadette. I can't tell you how much that pissed us off. Think of this as payback."

"You bastards. I will get you for this."

"Come to think of it," said Lucy, "this isn't even real jail. You get to talk to us! We're much better company than a bunch of gangbangers in prison. You get to be with civilized human beings. It must be a big change for you."

"And," I said, "the meals are better."

"The meals suck," he said.

"Well yes, but they're better than prison food. Anything's better than that."

"How would you know?"

"Nails told me."

"Nails has been in prison?" asked Dread.

"Jail, not prison. The cops busted him a couple of times."

"He's a pussy too. Thinks he's a fighter."

"You don't know, do you."

"Know what?" asked Dread.

"Yeah, what?" asked Lucy.

"Nails was a top middleweight. He beat some good boxers on the way up, had a record of 22 and 2. People thought he could've been a champion."

"No shit," said Lucy.

Dread just stared.

"What happened?" asked Lucy. "Somebody beat him bad?"

"Nope. Car accident. He was driving, some drunk plowed through a four-way stop and T-boned him. Killed his wife and kid, 'cause they were on that side of the car. Messed him up too. Broke a lot of bones in his face. The surgeons put him back together but the boxing commission said he could never fight again. Too dangerous."

"Aw man," said Lucy, "that really sucks."

"I know. I thought he was just another homeless guy who hung out in front of the building, so I bought him breakfast whenever he showed up. I knew him six months before I ever knew his name, then I Googled him. Old Nails was a helluva boxer."

"Damn," said Lucy. "Now he's a drunk?"

"Sometimes. He'll stay sober awhile, then he'll get sad and go on a bender. Stay drunk for a week or two. I've never seen it, but I talked to a couple other street guys and they say he's quite a handful. Put a couple guys in the hospital."

"He picked a fight?"

"No. A couple skinheads thought it would be fun to get drunk and beat up homeless people. They picked the wrong guy. Cops found them unconscious and called an ambulance."

Dread sat there on his mat, glued to the conversation. I could see a little respect in his eyes.

"Wow," said Lucy.

"Yeah," I said. "Dread here thinks he's a badass, but Nails could tear him apart."

"Bullshit," said Dread, but I didn't think his heart was in it.

Lucy and I left awhile later, leaving Dread with his thoughts.

# CHAPTER 21

"DREAD," SAID BERNADETTE, "Why are you such an asshole."

"Why are you such a bitch?"

"I asked first."

"Well, Bern, I'm a guy. You push me too far and I'm going to react."

"By react, you mean beating up people."

"If that's what it takes."

"So you think I pushed you into beating me up?"

"Yeah. You got on my nerves and it pissed me off. You let me out of this fucking cage and I'll do it again."

"Sure. That sounds like a plan. You know what's sad? You're not a bad musician. How the hell can you like music and be such a terrible person?"

"I don't like music. I just played it to get chicks."

"You learned to play bass just to get groupies?"

"Hey, it worked. I got you, didn't I?"

"Maybe at first, but I stayed around for the cocaine."

"I found that out later. If I knew coke brought women I never would've picked up the bass."

"So it was all just about women."

"Oh hell yes. I love sex. You should know that."

"Really? You weren't very good at it."

Dread laughed.

"Nice try. I heard you moaning. Heard you hit those screaming orgasms. You loved it."

"Shit, Dread, I think I had one orgasm all the time we were together. I'm just a good actress. Back then I would've faked death if I knew it would get me a line of blow."

"Don't matter to me. I got off, and that's all that matters. You're just another chick."

"Yeah I am. And I could be the last chick you ever see."

"I'll get out of here. Trust me."

"How's that working so far? Got your escape plans all worked out? You digging a hole through that plywood? Going to get skinny and slide down the toilet pipe?"

"My boys will find me. Or the police. You can't keep me here forever."

"We're doing good so far. Yep. I could be the last chick you ever see. And you're going to regret the stuff you did to me, forever."

"Not a chance. Come over here and I'll teach you to disrespect me."

"Oh Dread, Dread..," said Bernadette, "you ain't punching nobody ever again."

"How you going to stop me?"

"Well, I could chop off your arms and legs. That would do it."

"You come near me and I'll kill you."

"It was just a thought. Sometimes I think about that at night and it gives me comfort. I wonder if you'd be so mean with no arms or legs."

"Dream on, bitch, nobody's touching me."

"Not yet. But you got to eat, and I could slip something into your food, knock you out, sneak in with a butcher knife . . . ."

"Fuck you. Nobody's touching me."

"Maybe not yet but my friends are getting really tired of you. Makes you think, doesn't it? Like tonight after dinner, just think about me sneaking something into your food. Think of me with a knife. Then sleep well . . . ."

"Get out of here! I don't want you in here!"

"You know, Dread, I think I'll stay awhile. Meditate. I'll just sit over there by the wall and be quiet awhile. Let my mind be peaceful. You should try it."

"No way you're going to have peace, bitch. I'll sing my heart out, I'll scream at you."

"Let's try it and see how long you can do that."

Bernadette walked over to the wall, sat cross-legged and closed her eyes. Dread sang at the top of his voice, using swear words instead of lyrics. Bernadette sat. Dread sang and yelled. Still she sat quietly. Finally he could keep it up no longer and lay down on his pad. She sat a long time.

When she was done, she got up and walked back to the chair and sat down.

"Dread," she said, "I'm sorry. All that stuff about a knife? I could never do that. It goes against everything I've learned. I want to be peaceful now and live quietly."

"You had me fooled. I think you're an evil, lying bitch."

"Well damn. If you're right, then you got to keep worrying I might fly off the handle. Dose your food. Get a knife. That would be awful. I have to go now. Sleep well."

She left the room, happy with her psycho act. Payback.

# CHAPTER 22

DREAD SAT ON the pad in his cell. Nails was punching the heavy bag. He was drunk. He'd been gone for over a week and looked terrible. He smelled terrible too. His hair was lank and matted, his shoes had holes in them and his toes stuck out. His pants were grimy and his tee shirt was a filthy shade of gray. He hadn't shaved. He staggered around the bag, punching occasionally, weak punches that lacked the zip and power of a couple weeks ago.

"You look like shit," said Dread from inside his cell.

"Yeah. I know."

"How drunk are you?"

"Real drunk. I like being drunk. It cleans my brain. I can't remember shit."

"I can't believe you were a big-time fighter."

"Maybe I wasn't. I'm drunk. I don't remember."

"Monte said you were high in the rankings."

"Who's Monte?"

"Man, you are drunk."

"I know who Monte is," Nails mumbled. "I just don't care."

"Why don't you keep on drinking? You get lost out there on the streets and there's one less jailer to worry about."

"I might. But not this time. This one's over."

"How do you know?"

"I just do. How long has it been?"

"You been gone about eight days."

"That should be good enough. Clean out some memories, kill some brain cells."

"Where do you go when you're drinking?"

"How the fuck do I know? I just wander."

"How do you get the money for booze?"

"That's the funny part. I got some money in the bank, got an ATM card no one knows about."

"No shit? You got money and you blow it on cheap booze?"

"Sometimes I blow it on expensive booze. I've got that stashed around town too. I pour good wine into Blue Nun bottles so nobody knows. Sometimes it looks like I'm drinking Mad Dog wine and I got good brandy in that bottle."

"You're fucking weird."

"Everyone's weird, some just handle it better."

Nails punched the bag some more, staggering around it in a parody of a fighter's stance.

"I'm weird," he said as he punched, "but I'm not beat-up-woman weird. That's worse than being a drunk."

"You don't know shit. You don't know where I came from, what I had to deal with, how bitches screwed up my life."

"Oh poor me," said Nails.

"You don't know."

"Yeah I don't. And I don't care. Everyone's got a story. Every drunk in town can tell you about their tough childhood. Momma left, Dad left, stepdad abused them, uncle Harry was a pervert, the priest cornered them by the altar—everyone's got a story. I heard 'em all."

"Maybe, but that doesn't mean they're not real."

"Oh hell, they're all real and they don't mean shit. You either rise up or you fall."

"Looks like you fell all the way."

"Yeah but I don't make excuses. Nobody did it to me and I don't walk around blaming my old man or my mom or the full moon or whatever shit you're going to lay on me."

"You don't know."

"Right. And I don't want to know. You're an asshole, you don't want to change, and you're worse than a wino. I'm a drunk but I never beat up a woman."

"I don't think you could in your condition."

"Yeah, but in a couple days I'll be okay. You won't. You'll still be a pissant."

"Shit old man, I could take you right now."

"You sure could. Two days from now I'd rip your head off."

"Big talk when I'm in this cage."

"Maybe I'll come in the cage with you. Lock the door, see who comes out. You like close fighting? You like punching in the clinches? I was pretty good at that."

"I'd rip you up."

"Someday we'll have to try it. If Bernadette doesn't cut you up first. Lot of anger in that woman."

"She won't do that."

"I don't know. It would be so easy. A little roofie in your sandwich and you'd be laid out cold. She wouldn't even have to come into the cell if she had a long knife, like a machete."

"She said she wouldn't do that."

"Okay. Then that'll never happen right? Just 'cause you beat her up and threatened her kids. Women always forgive stuff like that. If I were you I'd hope she never pops a few shots of tequila and flies into a drunken rage."

"You can't let her do that."

"Why not? You're an evil fuck and it would solve all our

problems. You're a pain in the ass and we're all getting tired of it."

"You're not bad people. You wouldn't let her do that."

"Ever killed anyone?"

"No, but I've put some in the hospital. Why?"

"Monte has."

"Monte? That wimpy guy? No chance in hell."

"I'm the only one who knows, except for you, and if you tell people they'll think you're an idiot. Quiet guy like Monte? The guy in suits and glasses? The rich kid? No way."

"You're saying he killed someone?"

"Maybe. Maybe I'm just goofing with you. Some day you'll know but it might be too late."

"How about you?" asked Dread. "You ever killed anyone?"

"Nope. Just beat 'em fair and square. Too bad they don't let you fight women in the ring. You could've been a champ."

"Quit ragging on that. She had it coming."

"What'd she do, bruise your little ego? Make fun of your dick?"

"You don't know. She could drive a guy crazy. Nagging all the time, pissing me off."

"Oooh boy, that must've been so hard to take. Let's see, I had guys trying to beat the shit out of me, you had a nagging girlfriend. Which is a better reason to fight?"

"Fuck you. She asked for it."

"Yeah, like you're asking for it now. I wouldn't push this when I'm sober 'cause I might take you up on it. Better yet, I might get Bernadette some roofies for your food. Watch her go to work on you."

Nails went back to punching the bag, trying to sweat out the booze, trying to sober up. This was the hardest part of his blackout benders, coming back to reality. In time he went up to the penthouse guest room, took off his clothes and stood under the shower for a long time. Then he staggered out into the other room, and lay down on the floor, naked and shivering. Monty found him there and covered him up, put a pillow under his head.

## CHAPTER 23

LUCY HAD THE plans for the houseboat all drawn up and they were beautiful. Three bedrooms, three baths, a chef's kitchen, big living room and dining room, it was going to be a masterpiece. Lots of designer touches, lots of bay windows looking out on Lake Union, it was her best effort by far.

She took the plans to Charles Bledsoe's hotel and met with him in the bar early that afternoon. It was almost empty, so they commandeered a big table in the back and poured over them. Like all overbearing people he wanted to make changes. Some were okay, some were stupid. She pointed out the stupid ones and told him why. Immediately she realized she could've been more diplomatic.

"I'm sorry," she said. "I've been working long hours on these plans and thought sure you'd like them. Let's go over them again and see if we can compromise with these changes you want."

"This is not a negotiation," he said. "I'm paying for the houseboat, I want these changes and it's your job to put them in. Just do it."

"Well shit," said Lucy. "There's no way in hell your idea for the dining room-kitchen arrangement is going to work. It can't be done. So no, I can't do that."

He did not take it well, and fired her on the spot.

I found her raging in my office and slowly I drew out the story. I had worried about this, as I knew Charles was rich, impulsive and sometimes impossible to work with. During the embezzlement investigation he'd almost fired me three or four times and I'd come to dislike the man intensely. He was good-looking, in a silver-haired banker sort of way, but you could see a self-importance and arrogance underneath the smooth exterior. There were times I wanted to let his money manager skip town with the cash.

Lucy was heartbroken. This was the biggest job of her career and now it was gone. Also, the money she'd promised to finance our adventure was no longer there. I tried to console her, but I wasn't doing well. We sat awhile and I did some heavy thinking. Finally, I told her to go get Bernadette. When they got back I motioned for them to sit down and made a call. I had a plan.

"Charles," I said, "we have to talk."

"No we don't. Your contractor screwed up the plans and disrespected me. She's done."

"Are you sure about that?"

"Positive."

"Absolutely?"

"Yes, damn it. She's fired."

"Do you mind if I put you on speakerphone?"

"No problem. The more the merrier."

"Okay. So let's be clear. You fired Lucy and you don't want the plans?"

"That's right. They didn't fulfill my expectations."

"She put a lot of time and effort into those plans."

"I don't care. I want no part of them. She screwed up."

"Well that's great." I could hear a startled gasp.

"What do you mean it's great?"

"Lucy drew up the plans here in my office and I've been fascinated by them. I never thought of owning a houseboat, but this . . . this idea is really intriguing. Now that you don't want the plans, I think I'm going to use them myself. I'm sure I can find a spot on Lake Union."

I could feel him start to wonder.

"You're not serious."

"Deadly serious. Not only that, I had a couple architect friends check out the plans and they're impressed too. I want to build it, live in it, and if I don't like it I'm sure I can make a big profit if I sell it. I can't lose."

"Now wait a minute, Monte. I paid to have those plans drawn up so I think by rights they still belong to me."

"I don't think so. You're on speakerphone and I've got witnesses here. You said you fired Lucy and you don't want the plans. Call me crazy, but I think they belong to her now."

"I'll fight that. I'll take you to court."

"You could, but you do realize I'm not some lightweight you can threaten with a lawsuit. I'd be willing to bet my pockets are just as deep as yours and I'll be in it for the long haul. We're talking years in court."

"Damn it, Monte, you can't do this to me."

"Let me see. You can have Lucy do great work for you, get all her hopes up, and then blow her dreams, but I can't take some plans you don't even want? Is that what you're saying?"

"Now wait."

"You wait. In a few months I'm going to have the nicest, most innovative houseboat on Lake Union and you're going to have jack shit. I think we're talking Architectural Digest here."

"Monte, Monte, I may have acted hastily here."

"You sure did."

"We can find some sort of compromise, can't we?"

"I can't think of any way to do that. You screwed over Lucy and you pissed me off. I think we're done here."

"Wait! Come on Monte, what if I hire Lucy back? What if I let her build the houseboat?"

Over my shoulder I could see Lucy and Bernadette high fiving each other.

"I don't know, Charles. You could just fire her again and I'd never have a chance to build it."

"I'll give her a solid contract. No opting out on my part. She'll have final say on the design and construction."

"You're sure? I've seen you change your mind before. Make a deal and back out."

"You can check the contract, take it to your lawyers. Make sure it's unbreakable."

"I would definitely do that, but it'll cost me."

"Okay, okay, I'll pay the legal fees."

"You sure? You can back out now for free."

"No, I want the houseboat. Will she do it?"

"What about the trauma she just went through? How will you make up for that?"

"You're pushing it, Monte"

"You bet I am. You treated her like dirt."

Charles paused. He thought about it.

"Okay, you win. What works for you?"

"A raise of some sort. Maybe fifteen percent."

"Five. I can't do fifteen it's too much."

"We'll split the difference. Ten."

"Done. I won't forget this, Monte."

"Neither will I. You tried to screw over my friend. Send the new contract over and I'll have my lawyers go over it. Remember, no slight of hand or we're going to court."

"Okay, okay. Can Lucy come back to work tomorrow?"

"I'll check with her and let you know. One last thing, Charles. You sure on this? You won't let me have those plans?"

"Not a chance, Monte. That houseboat is going to be glorious."

"Okay. Talk to you later."

We hung up. Lucy and Bernadette were laughing and dancing around the floor. The kids looked bewildered.

When they'd calmed down, Lucy looked at me.

"Would you really have built that houseboat?"

"Oh hell yes, just to spite him. I never liked Charles."

# CHAPTER 24

LUCY AND BERNADETTE were sitting in the office, having put the kids down for their naps. They sat, drinking coffee, peaceful.

"When did you know you were a lesbian?" asked Bernadette.

"When did you know you were a drug addict?" asked Lucy.

They laughed.

"I know you play for the other team," said Lucy, "although after two years with Dread I will never understand that. He should've put you off men forever."

"You'd think so, wouldn't you. On the other hand, those women in prison put a damper on the whole lesbian thing. They were as bad as he was."

"Shit girl," said Lucy, "I can't believe the life you've led."

"Back to you. You had two big brothers, right?

"Right."

"So they protected you."

"There were two sides to that. They were both jocks, so if anyone picked on me at school I had protection. But around the house we played all sports and I didn't get any favors. None of that girly stuff. I played tackle football in the yard, basketball in the driveway, and catcher in baseball season."

"You were a tomboy."

"Yeah, and I liked it. My mom worried about me."

"Did you date boys?"

"Oh sure. I even had a boyfriend in high school but it never felt right."

"Did you and him do the nasty?"

"Yeah. Once. I think I really hurt his feelings. He was a nice guy and he tried so hard to be gentle and loving and I still cried afterwards and it just felt wrong. I broke up with him a couple days later and he thought he'd screwed up, so I swore him to secrecy and told him I liked girls more than boys. I think it was a big relief for him.

"So you had this boy thing that didn't work out and that's when you knew, right?"

"I think I always knew. I never stared at boys or got giggly. But I fell in love with my English teacher, Miss Whalen. All the boys did too. She was really hot."

"How old were you?" asked Bernadette.

"I was a sophomore in high school. I played soccer and basketball and watching girls in the locker room was really strange for me. That's the thing about being gay, you get to see all the desirable people naked. Gay boys get to go in the boy's shower. Straight boys never get to go in the girl's showers."

"I never thought of that," said Bernadette. "That's not fair at all! I never got to see naked boys. That's discrimination!"

They laughed.

"Sex is so confusing."

"It sure is," said Bernadette. "So did you have any girlfriends in high school?"

"I was afraid. I didn't know what my parents would think, and I figured my brothers would freak out. Jocks aren't the most liberated people on the planet, especially in high school."

"So you covered it up?"

"Yeah. It was so scary. If I approached a girl and she turned out to be straight, word would get out and I'd be the butt of every joke in school. I'm sure the other gay girls were scared of the same thing. How would you know? Back then, girls weren't coming out in high school, especially not in Idaho."

"That's kind of crappy. So you never got to take a girl to the prom or make out under the bleachers?"

"I wouldn't say never . . . ."

"Aha! So you did find a girl!"

"More like she found me. She was one of the soccer players and one day she sat down at my table in the cafeteria. Some of the jocks were being rowdy and she said, 'Boys are such pigs.'"

"And you said?"

I wasn't sure what to say. I loved my brothers, but I just said, "Yeah, boys are pigs."

The girl said, "You ever dated boys?"

And I said, "I had a boyfriend for awhile but it felt wrong. I didn't like it."

"She smiled, and right then we both knew."

"Ah," Bernadette laughed, "you found a soulmate!"

"Yeah. That afternoon we went to the park after school and found a place way back in the trees. No prying eyes. We kissed and touched each other and I'd never felt feelings like that before."

"Okay," said Bernadette. "We get to the good part. Did you have wild sex? Lots of creamy white thighs and heaving breasts?"

"I forgot to tell you, she was black. I think hers was the only black family in Sandpoint. Maybe in all of Idaho. Back then Idaho was the whitest state in the union. And she was so gorgeous. The the only creamy white thighs were mine. We went together for almost a year and nobody knew."

"Nobody? Really? In high school? How the hell did you pull that off?"

"Oh we were so discreet. It was a big part of the thrill. We were like super spies, sneaking around, finding secret hideouts. It was the most exciting thing that ever happened to me."

"That is so cool. My high school romances seem really tacky compared to that. How did it end?"

"That was the worst part. Her family moved away. Her dad got a job in California and it was real sudden. One day she was there, two weeks later she was gone. I cried for a week."

"Did you stay in touch?"

"We did for awhile, but you know teenagers. We moved on to other things."

"Other girls?"

"Well that too. Then I went to the UW and there were lesbian groups and gay rights and I came out in my freshman year."

"Did your family freak out?"

"Not a bit! We all were home for Thanksgiving and I made this big announcement. I expected my parents to be shocked and uncomfortable and my brothers to be worse. But they all laughed and said they'd known for years. Everybody hugged me and we drank beer and got rowdy and played football in the front yard and it was one of the great days of my life."

"How about your little sister?"

"Oh she was fine. She was the girly one in the family and this meant she had a corner on all that stuff. My mom was so happy she was straight. It was a win-win for everyone."

"Well shit," said Bernadette. "I was hoping for a little more drama than that. Ever think about that girl in high school?"

"Every day. She was the best."

"What was her name?"

Lucy got a dreamy look in her eye. "Annette."

# CHAPTER 25

THEY PAUSED, BERNADETTE soaking in Lucy's story.

"Okay," Lucy said, "your turn. Where'd you grow up?"

"Spokane. And my parents didn't split up and I wasn't abused by a weird uncle. I had a pretty normal life."

"How'd you get named Bernadette?"

"It was my grandmother's name. I hated it for years because it was so old-fashioned. But now I'm used to it."

"Brothers and sisters?"

"One sister. Older. Straight A student, cheerleader, beautiful, everything you could want in a girl."

"Wow. Tough act to follow."

"It really was. But she wasn't prissy about it. We had great times together."

"Where is she now?"

"She studied law. She's back in Washington D.C., clerking for a Senator. Just got married to a young congressman from Maine."

"Wow, impressive. What were you like?"

"Chubby. I loved 3 Musketeers and Cocoa Puffs. My mom tried hard to get me to eat better but I found ways."

"So you were the fat kid?"

"Such a cliché. I wasn't fat, like really fat, but I was chubby. Round face, no waist, the usual. And I wasn't an A student. I didn't like books, so I hovered around C's. I did okay in art and I liked computers. Games. I liked computer games."

"Uh oh. Girl nerd alert."

"Yeah, kind of like that, all through grade school and middle school."

"How about high school?"

"Big trouble. I blossomed. I was the first girl to have real boobs. And I grew four inches taller and the fat went away. I had cheekbones! I had a waist! I had long legs!"

"Uh oh, so you morphed from nerd girl to boy magnet."

"Right, and I had no clue how to handle it. My sister tried to help me because she'd been popular all her life, but I didn't handle it well at all."

"Don't tell me. You got pregnant."

"No, that was the only thing I didn't do. My sister got me on the pill and it saved me from having a kid because I was definitely screwing around."

"Just to be popular?"

"No. I liked boys. They totally turned me on."

"Any particular kind of boy?"

"Not jocks. They were too obvious. I wanted the brooding outlaw types, the goths and the troubled kids. I'd been a nerd! I identified with the outcasts. We had stuff to talk about."

"I can see that. And you had lots of sex?"

"Not lots, but I did like it. For one thing, I was good at it. You've got to realize, I'd never been good at anything in my life. I was a C student, I wasn't a prom queen, but when it came to sex, I was gangbusters. I made guys feel like kings and I had orgasms that blew me away. I loved my body!

"Did you have a boyfriend?"

"I had a few boyfriends. I'm not sure I achieved slut status but I was in the running."

"That sounds dangerous. Any STD's?"

"No. My sister had given me the talk. I carried condoms and I made boys wear them. I did get the crabs once."

"The crabs? No shit?"

"They were awful! I started itching down there and couldn't figure out why. Then I got these little black dots in my pubes. One day I was in the bathtub, scratching, and I picked at one of those black spots and it came up in my fingernail. And it was moving!! I damn near screamed."

"What'd you do?"

"I called my sister. She was at college. She talked me down and told me to go to a pharmacy and get some of that blue ointment. I got it and it worked."

"Good to know. Did you know who gave them to you?"

"I had a pretty good idea. So I gave him the rest of the ointment and broke up. It was too bad, 'cause he was a sweet guy. Just not big on cleanliness."

"What'd you do after high school?"

"My grades were bad so all I could get into was community college in Olympia. It was a party school and I liked that. I loved dancing. I loved the way my body moved. That's how I met Dread."

"That blows my mind. How'd you end up with a loser like him?"

"He was my type. Musician, outlaw, loner—we had lots to talk about. At first, he was a nice guy, treated me okay. I went to gigs with him, danced all night, hung out with the other musicians, drank, smoked dope, I loved it. Rock and Roll!"

"Sounds like fun."

"Yeah, but it changed. The band started doing other drugs. Ecstasy, hash, coke, crack, whatever showed up at the gigs."

"So you did them too?"

"Sure. That's when I fell in love with cocaine and Dread

found if he had coke he could make me do anything he wanted. Typical. Stupid girl addict. He even tried to share me with other guys. I wasn't that far gone, so I refused and he punched me out. After awhile he would just hit me for no reason."

"Fuck me. And you couldn't walk away?"

"How? I had no money, and he had coke."

"How about your parents? Or your sister? Couldn't you call them?"

"Oh sure. Hi Mom and Dad, I'm a junkie whore and my boyfriend beats me up. Mind if I come home for awhile? I couldn't face that."

"And your sister?"

"Naw. She was in D.C., had a great career. How would she like a doper slut like me showing up? I couldn't do that either."

"How'd you break away?"

"I sure didn't plan it. Dread and the guys were playing this tough bar. Some guy wanted to dance and I wanted to dance so we hit the floor and boogied. Well, the guy's girlfriend was drunk and came at me in a rage. Someone yelled "Girl-fight!" and the floor cleared while we went at it. I guess I was tired of getting beat up and I just exploded. They had to pull me off her and then the cops came. A woman cop started acting real snarky so I punched her too. Not a good idea."

"No. Not good."

"I got busted for assault and resisting arrest and got two years in the women's prison down in Shelton."

"That seems excessive."

"I had a lousy lawyer. Court appointed. He showed up drunk."

"Well shit."

"Yeah. I couldn't get drugs in prison because I was new and didn't have money, so I was having withdrawals in my cell. My cellmate hated all the noise and throwing up so she slapped me and told me to shut up. Big mistake on her part. I was sick, I'd hit rock bottom, I'd been beaten up, and I just went crazy. The guards had to pull me off her and they threw me in the hole. Six weeks in solitary."

"That's awful."

"No. It was the best thing that ever happened to me. In a couple weeks I'd gone through withdrawals and realized my life was crap. There was nothing to do, so I meditated. I didn't even know how to meditate, but I'd seen kids do it in college. I sat on the floor and counted my breaths. I don't think you're supposed to do it that way, but that's what I did. I got so I could meditate for an hour, relax, and then do another. I did it for the rest of the time in the hole and when they put me back in a cell I did it there too. I know my cellmate wanted to give me shit, but she knew I'd gone postal on my last cellie so she left me alone. Every day I meditated."

"No shit."

"Hey, it was prison. There wasn't much else to do and it passed the time. That and meetings. I went to meetings."

"Did it work?"

"Yeah. I got calm. I got strong. Then I found out I was three months pregnant. Hard to believe a drug addict would forget to take the pill, right? I had my babies in the prison infirmary and later got out on some sort of compassionate parole. I worked all kinds of jobs—dish washing, janitor, part time secretary, fast food—anything I could find. Nails heard about me, told Monte, and here I am."

"Amazing. Do you still want cocaine?"

"Every day. But I go to meetings and meditate and do one day at a time."

"That's an amazing story."

"Well, yours was pretty good too. I'm happy we're friends."

"Me too," said Lucy.

They sat quietly for awhile, watching the kids sleep.

"There's one thing I don't understand," said Bernadette.

"What's that?"

"Why are you trying to bring down a bad guy? That's really off the wall. You must have some really strong reason, right?"

"Yeah, I do, but I haven't told anyone."

"Fair enough. You don't have to tell me either."

"Thanks."

They sat. Then Lucy said, "Do you really want to know?"

"Of course. I'm nosy as hell."

"And we're friends, right? And fellow criminals?"

"Right."

"Remember Annette?"

"The girl from high school?"

"Yeah. I lied when I said we lost touch. We emailed each other all through high school. We dreamed of getting back together. Then she joined the military and trained as an EMT, got stationed in Iraq."

"Oh man, that doesn't sound good."

"It wasn't. She was in a Humvee and it got taken out by an IED. No one survived. I didn't find out until three days later. They found our emails on her computer and her commanding officer called me. My beautiful Annette was dead. Gone forever."

"Oh Lucy . . . ,"

Lucy was in tears now and she folded into Bernadette's arms. Bernadette lost it too. They held each other a long time. Finally, Lucy spoke.

"I'm sorry, I thought I was cried out."

"Grief is weird," said Bernadette, still holding her.

"It is."

They were quiet for awhile. Lucy broke the silence.

"I was heartbroken and really pissed off. Stupid fucking war, stupid fucking assholes who send young people off to die. I was so angry. And there was a funeral in California and I went and I laid flowers on Annette's coffin, and cried and wanted to scream in rage. And there was nothing I could do. No way I could go to Iraq and find the people who planted that bomb."

"It kept coming back to me, that terrible, terrible waste of my beautiful Annette. Then, in one week, I got that big houseboat commission and I saw Monte's name in the paper, how he'd cracked open the embezzlement case, and I thought, I want to destroy some of the evil in the world. I want revenge."

Bernadette sat, thoughtful. "It makes sense to me," she said. "A blow for the good guys."

"Yeah. One for the Gipper."

"Who the hell is the Gipper?"

Lucy, through her tears, laughed.

"My dad was a Notre Dame fan."

# CHAPTER 26

BERNADETTE FELL INTO a routine where she would meditate in the prison room during the kids' nap time. Usually it was the only time she spent with Dread. So that time was hers. Every day.

At first, Dread had tried to disrupt her. She would go in, set down her cushion, and sit cross-legged, her hands on her knees. It wasn't a pure lotus position, but it was the one she'd adopted in prison and it worked for her. She knew nothing of Buddhism, other than a few fragments she'd picked up, and she'd never studied meditation. She just did it her own way, counting the breaths until she got to her goal.

After his attempts to bother her failed, Dread gave up and just went about his business. Napping, reading comic books. There was no TV during Bernadette's time. Sometimes he exercised, doing sit-ups and push-ups and a bogus version of martial arts that he'd picked up from TV. Sometimes he shadowboxed. Bernadette just sat there. After the first hour she would take a five-minute break and stretch and walk around. Dread would try to talk to her, but she remained silent. Then she would sit down and do another hour.

After a few weeks of this, Dread could see she was stronger than anything he could throw at her so he decided to beat her at her own game.

"You think that's a big deal? You think you're some sort of guru, with your Buddha stuff? Anyone can do that shit. I could do it longer than you if I wanted. I'm tougher than you, my brain's tougher than you. Come on, damn it, let's see who can do this the longest."

Bernadette said one sentence, the first she'd said in quite awhile.

"I don't compete."

Dread sneered. "Fuck yes you don't compete, 'cause you know I'll win. I was always better than you."

Bernadette just went back for her second hour of sitting.

The next day, when she walked in to sit, Dread was waiting. She sat on her cushion and he sat on his pad. She assumed her position and he assumed his.

They sat.

After fifteen minutes, Dread was squirming. After twenty minutes he opened his eyes and said, "This is stupid."

He thought he saw a slight smile on Bernadette's lips and it pissed him off. He lay down on his bunk and swore he'd never do that again.

But the next day he woke up thinking he couldn't let her beat him. Not a chance. If he could spend hours learning bass guitar, he could sit still. That day he made thirty minutes before he started swearing and lay down again on his bunk. Defeated.

The next day he didn't sit at all. Fuck it. He wasn't going for that kumbaya bullshit. He did exercises and shadowboxed. Bernadette appeared not to notice.

Dread was feeling something else too. He was noticing how good she looked. Better than she ever had when she was with him. She was healthy, and calm, and most of all, she was not needy or submissive. She was strong. She never tried to look good. She wore sweatpants and a sweatshirt. She never wore makeup and her hair was natural. In spite of all that, she looked better than before and he felt an attraction to her. He cursed himself. She was trying to break him and that was not going to happen. The bitch was not going to get the better of him. Fuck that. He would show her.

The next day when she sat, he did too. He lasted forty minutes. He opened his eyes and cursed when he saw her still sitting. He got up, stretched his legs and arms, and lay down. When she started her second hour, he did too. She counted her breaths. He slowly did the lyrics of every song he ever knew, one word with each breath. When that didn't work, he cursed her, very slowly, trying to take up the time. He did mental bass runs and scales, anything to keep sitting as long as she did. He made it through the second hour. She stood up, said nothing, took her cushion and left the room. Dread lifted his arms in silent triumph. Yes! He'd shown her!

Every day after that, he matched her, hour for hour but while she counted breaths, he dwelt on anger, cursing, reliving fights, going over the things that had messed up his life, imagining screaming bass lines to thrash metal lyrics, taking thundering trips on his Harley—anything to keep his mind occupied while he sat there and matched her breath for breath. He would not break. He would beat this woman at her own game.

The days went on, and he found it harder and harder to sustain his rage. Sometimes he'd wind down and just breathe, take a little vacation from his violent dreams, but then he'd get angry at himself. No! He would not let her turn him into a wuss! None of this hippie peace and love bullshit. He'd go back to violence, dreaming of pool hall fights and knock-down, drag-out battles with his stepdad, screaming rages with his mom, both of them alcoholics, both of them mean.

Sometimes, sitting there, he would shiver with anger, but he wouldn't open his eyes, he wouldn't let Bernadette know.

He began to look forward to the sitting. It was a competition. It was something he could win, sitting in this fucking cell with these lunatics keeping him caged up. He could beat her. He would sit longer than her. That's right. Two fucking hours was nothing. He'd do two and a half. Maybe three. Show that bitch.

Somewhere, in reincarnation land, the Buddha was laughing.

# CHAPTER 27

NAILS ATTACKED DREAD from another direction. His manhood. Dread was actually a tough guy from a tough background. He was biker tough. He could take pain and he could dish it out. Give him a motorcycle chain and a bar fight and he could kick ass.

Nails figured that out early and never challenged him. He was fascinated by Dread and this whole crazy process, so in his sober periods he would stay in Monte's penthouse. He'd come into Dread's room in the mornings and workout. First he'd skip rope. After a blackout bender he could barely do three or four minutes. The liquor always took a big toll on his conditioning and he looked like an old man barely getting his feet off the ground, grunting with the effort.

After that he'd shadowbox, dancing around the room, throwing jabs, hooks, uppercuts, bobbing and weaving. But again he was old and slow. A massive hangover sapping his energy. He'd do it till he could do no more and then he'd sit and get his energy, what there was of it, back. Finally, he'd punch the heavy bag. There was no snap to his punches, no power.

But each day he'd get stronger. Dread would watch as the rope skipping would get faster and longer, the shadowboxing quicker, and the heavy bag begin to take punishment. He saw that Nails knew what he was doing. Sometimes they talked.

"Why you doin' that old man? You never gonna fight again."

"I know. This is just my life. And you know something? I keep learning. I watch old fights and see new moves, little things, and I want to try them out. There's no reason, I just like it."

"That's stupid, learning something you'll never use."

"I agree. I never said I was smart."

"Who's your favorite fighter?"

"Now?"

"Yeah. Now. I don't know the old guys."

"Pacquiao. That guy is amazing. Punches in bunches. And the way he moves . . . , it's like watching a dancer out there, coming at you from all directions. Ever seen him fight?"

"I think so. Little guy, right? Filipino?"

"Yeah, that's him."

"Could you have fought him? When you were good?"

Nails laughed, "Oh I could've fought him, but he would've beat the crap out of me. I was pretty good but he's a once-in-a-lifetime guy. He's like Ali or Sugar Ray Robinson."

"So you weren't that good."

"No one's that good."

"But you still keep trying. Why the hell do that?"

"I have no idea. I just like it. It's a science. An art. Nobody learns it all. It's like a puzzle you can't figure out."

"I just wanted to beat up people," said Dread.

"I knew lots of guys like you. You find them in bars all over the world. Tough guys."

"That's right. I am tough."

"Yeah, you probably are. But there's always someone tougher. That's how it works. One day you run into him and bam, lights out. If you're lucky you don't come out a vegetable. Especially in bar fights. You can get cut by bottles, brained by pool cues, get your insides messed up when they kick you . . . . They can fuck you up for life."

"Yeah, but that's the chance you take. It's like cage fighting. You're betting your life."

"You think boxing's not like that? I know boxers who can't talk. Can't make a compete sentence. Their life is over and they don't know it. I never would've boxed if I could've played something like basketball or baseball. Or better yet, been a smart guy, like a doctor or lawyer. I boxed because that was all I was good at."

"And look where it got you. You're a bum."

"Boxing didn't do that. I did. I gave up."

"Why'd you give up?"

"I had a bad night."

"Monte told us about that."

"I lost everything. I lost my wife, my kid, my career, all because some drunk insurance salesman ran a stop sign. Everything was gone."

"Didn't you have family? Someone to turn to?"

"I did, but I couldn't go to them. I'd run away from home to go be a boxer. When I lost everything I couldn't go back and say, hey, I made a mistake. No, I had to live with it, whatever it was."

"How'd you get to be a boxer?"

"I sneaked out and fought Golden Gloves. Did about two years of that before I told my parents. They said no way I was going to be a fighter, I had to go to college. So I ran away from home. I was pretty much a street kid until the guy who owned the gym took me in."

"So he was a good guy?"

"Naw, he was a promoter, a scam artist and a cheat. He'd seen me fight Golden Gloves and realized he could make money off me. He stole money from me, he put me in fights I shouldn't have been in, but I always surprised him and everyone else. Only lost a couple of times and I never should've been in the ring with those guys. No, fuck him. He was evil."

"Where is he now?"

"In a coma. Someone mugged him in a dark alley and put him out for good."

"You know who did that?"

"I do. Someone with a big grudge and nothing to lose."

"No shit? You did him in?"

"Did I say that?"

"No."

"Let's leave it that way. Whoever did it shouldn't be proud. It didn't change a thing."

"Can you teach me to box?"

"Why, so you can beat up women?"

"I won't beat up women."

"Right, and I won't get drunk again. Face it, Dread, you're a mean bastard and that's not going to change. Why should I give you more tools to hurt people?"

"I could change."

"Nope. Not going to happen. You can't change mean. I know."

"So what's that? I'm judged? I'm going to be in this cage forever?"

"If I have a vote you are. I think we're doing a good thing for humanity. Besides, I've come to like Bernadette so in my book you're a fucking criminal. I'd throw away the key."

"Well fuck you. I can outlast all of you."

"Maybe. We'll see."

Nails went back to punching the heavy bag. His punches seemed harder.

## CHAPTER 28

THAT NIGHT WE held another meeting. We realized we were facing a bigger problem than we'd thought and it was getting in the way of Lucy's plan.

"Okay you guys," I said, "we have to face the truth here. We're farther away from our original idea than we were before we captured Dread. We were going to take down a criminal mastermind and instead we're blowing all our time on this small-time biker bass player. Any ideas?"

"The first thing is that we can't let Dread go." said Nails. "He's just as screwed up now as he was before we picked him up."

"I don't know," said Bernadette. "He is talking to us, and he's meditating with me. Maybe there's a possibility we can turn him around."

"Do you really think so?" said Lucy.

Bernadette grew quiet and then said, "No. I think Nails is right. Dread is dangerous. Also, as soon as he gets out he'll be back drinking and doing drugs. Any reforms would be out the window. I won't let him out to abuse someone else."

"So," said Lucy, "do we abandon our main plan and stick with Dread? Or do we build another cell and take two criminals off the streets?"

"You still want a big guy?" asked Nails. "You've seen the problems. First, we've got to kidnap a gangster and then we might have to keep him in a cell forever. We're no closer to changing a bad guy into a human being."

"I'm not so sure," I said. "It might be that we just didn't realize what a long process it's going to be. Learning anything takes years. Look at doctors, athletes, lawyers. They spend years learning their skills. Why shouldn't this be the same? We just have to first decide if we're in this for the long haul. What do you think?"

"I'm in," said Nails, "but I'm not giving up anything. I don't have things to do, places to go. My schedule is clear until . . . well, until I die. And this is just as good a way to spend my life as any."

"How about you, Bernadette? You've got your kids to think about."

"They're not a problem now," she said, "but what about the future? We have to get them in schools, I should have a real home for them, will they be in any danger? I've got to think of all that."

"This isn't all on you," I said. "We're in this together and that includes protecting the kids and seeing that they have a good life. It's complicated. Here's another thought. We're all single now, but what if we meet someone? How do you keep this a secret? Or do we let them in on our scheme? Keeping a secret with four people is scary enough, but what about five or six?"

"Hey Boss," said Lucy (she'd taken to calling me boss, along with Bernadette and Nails. I had the vague sense they used the term ironically). "Have you got some babe lined up? You been sneaking out to clubs?"

"No, I don't. And no, I haven't. This has taken up all my time. But that could change. I'm not a monk. So you see, the longer this takes the more complicated it becomes."

"AA," said Nails. "One day at a time."

"How do you know about AA?" asked Bernadette.

"Oh hell, I've been worked on by experts. God people, AA, Monte . . . ."

"Me?"

"Yeah you. I know you want me to clean up, get a real life. You're just easier about it."

"I never pressured you at all."

"Nope, and I appreciate it, but I know you want me to clean up. As you can see, you're my friend but so far Jack Daniels has edged you out."

"Damn. I've been beaten by a bottle."

"You can see why I don't have a lot of hope about changing these guys. I'm a sweetheart compared to gangsters and you couldn't even change me."

"Not yet," I said. "But you're faltering. Once you take that first shower . . . ."

"Dream on."

"Back to the problems at hand," I said. "Are we in it for the long haul? Do we still want to capture a real gangster?"

"I'm in," said Lucy. "Hell, it was my idea. I can't back out now."

"I'm in," said Bernadette. "You guys did a huge thing by taking Dread for me, so whatever you want to do, I'm your girl."

"I guess it's up to me," I said. "I'm in. But we've really got to think about how to make this process work, and how to make it work in a shorter time. Flipping people is a lot harder than flipping real estate."

"Call me crazy," said Lucy, "but wouldn't a smart person read up on all the literature about rehabilitation? Surely there must be someone out there who's had success."

"Good thought," I said. "Bernadette, why don't you and I take that on. Search the Internet and see if we can come up with something. Lucy, you've got full time work building the houseboat. Nails, you could work it from the other side. You must know people who have cleaned up their act."

"Maybe a couple, but they always hit rock bottom and finally get help."

I thought about that.

"Maybe that's the secret," I said. "Maybe these guys have to hit rock bottom. Instead of trying to change them, maybe we should get them as low as they can go."

"How?" asked Bernadette. "Give them all the drugs and liquor they can handle? Watch them disintegrate?"

"That's the usual process," said Nails. "But we don't want to be buying drugs. Maybe there's another rock bottom we can get them to. Some sort of despair that'll drive them to find a way out."

"Are we talking CIA stuff?" I asked. "Break them mentally? Torture?"

"No," said Lucy, "I didn't sign up for that."

We agreed. Waterboarding was out. As was loud music, flashing lights and all the other perversions used by the people keeping us free. We couldn't think of an answer, but we talked long into the night. There had to be a way.

# CHAPTER 29

BERNADETTE AND I studied. We spent our spare time on the Internet searching through literature on rehabilitation, cures for abusive people, how to deal with hardcore criminals and so on. Lucy and her crew worked on the construction of Charlie's houseboat. Nails asked around the homeless community, looking for tales of people who'd gotten back on their feet and how they did it. He also collected info on rehab centers, which was easy because most of his street friends had been to one or two. They figured the cure rate was under fifteen percent. Not encouraging.

The toddlers, Jake and Greg, did what toddlers do. Everything in the office was a toy to them, all of us were uncles and aunts, and they ate, napped and pooped. Come to think of it, they were a lot like Dread.

One night I went to bed in Dread's prison room. We had a cot set up there and now and then one of us slept comfortably about twenty feet outside the bars. The downside was we could hear clearly when he got up to piss in the middle of the night.

I was just nodding off, and again I thought about the mice studies, the ones with the cocaine and the cages.

I sat up in bed. This could be the answer!

The next morning, I called another meeting. I reminded them about the mouse experiments. Bernadette interjected.

"I think they were rats. Laboratory rats."

I nodded. "You're right. I forgot. Anyway, let's talk about Dread's life. Was he the rat in the first cage? The empty one? Did he have friends? Things to do?"

"He had the band," said Bernadette, "but I don't know if they were friends. Sometimes they hung out but mostly they were drinking and doing drugs."

"Do you know anything about his life as a kid?"

"Oh yeah. His dad ran away when he was like, five, and his mom was a drunk. His stepdad was a drunk. He lived in a trailer park. Had no friends in school unless you count the other rejects. He was lousy at sports, a bad student and girls thought he was ugly. I'd guess he was the rat in the empty cage. It sure explains the drugs and liquor."

"Then what?"

"The way I heard it, the other two rejects wanted to start a band and needed a bass player. Somehow he found a bass guitar and learned how to play it. The music was mostly loud and it wasn't complicated so he faked it until he figured it out. He's not a great musician but neither are they. They just crank it up and scream over it.

"So now he's in a band and he's got drugs and that's how he meets girls, but without the drugs I think he knows no girl wants to be with him. That's how he got me, but he knew I thought he was a bastard."

"Okay," I said. "Here's my crazy idea. What if we load him up with things to do, and make sure we're around him a lot? What if we get him good food too?"

"Sure," Nails said, "and beautiful women and hot tubs."

They laughed.

"Okay," I said, "there are limits, but that's my idea. Fill

up his life. Do you think it's crazy?"

"Not really," said Bernadette. "I went off on a tangent and watched stuff about dog whisperers and horse whisperers. People who take vicious animals and settle them down. There's two parts to it. Firmness and kindness. If we put stuff in for him to play with, and keep people in the room, that would take care of the kindness part. But how are you firm with someone in a cell already?"

"I know that one," said Nails. "You take the people out of the room. If he acts like an asshole, we leave. After awhile he'll get the picture."

"That's right!" said Bernadette. "And you have to do it immediately. One "fuck you" from him and we've got to be out of there."

"That makes sense," said Lucy, "I read about tribes where the greatest punishment is to ostracize one of the members. It's like those families where the dad says, 'She is no longer my daughter,' and no one can talk to her ever."

"That sounds harsh," said Nails.

"You haven't been around the gay community. It happens all the time. My son, gay? From this day forward I have no son. My daughter? same thing."

"I know it happens, but I don't understand how a parent could do that."

"Religion mostly. Homosexuality is a sin. God hates it. If your parents are really religious, good luck."

"Well that's just stupid," said Nails.

"Yes, but it happens all the time. Go down to any fundamentalist church and listen to them talk.

"If my daughter was gay she'd never set foot in this house again!" I've got tons of gay friends whose families have disowned them."

"How do they deal with it?"

"Oh we've got lots of support groups. And you can

always go to a gay bar. It's like family there."

"People are weird," said Nails. "Just weird."

"Back to the subject at hand," I said, "are we agreed on the plan with Dread?"

We agreed. We also agreed that it probably wouldn't work but at least we had a plan.

We then took up the other problem. Should we go after a real gangster?

We agreed we should, and that meant we had to build another cell. Location was no problem because the call center had taken up two adjoining offices and the other one was still vacant. While we were planning that and building the cell in the next office we would keep practicing on Dread.

I loved it. My life had been pretty purposeless up to now. As a trust fund guy, even the detective business was just something to keep life interesting. This was wonderfully crazy. And far more exciting.

## CHAPTER 30

THAT AFTERNOON, AFTER Bernadette and Dread did their meditations, we started moving stuff into the room around his cell. We arranged a curtain outside his cell that hid his toilet so he could ask to have it drawn when he used it. In his cell we put a Nerf basketball and hoop. We gave him an air mattress, quilt and a pillow. We gave him one of those blow-up chairs. Hard to make a weapon out of a blow-up chair. We gave him more comic books. We told him he could pick the TV shows. He was suspicious, but he certainly wasn't complaining.

We all sat down outside the cage and I spoke up.

"One other thing," I said. "Dread keeps asking for a bass guitar. Can we do that safely?"

"I don't know, boss," said Bernadette. "It would be pretty easy to turn it into a weapon."

"You mean he could hurt us with his music?"

They laughed. Dread didn't.

"No, I mean bass guitars are big and heavy. In his hands it could be dangerous."

"How about this?" I said. "We'll be in charge of it. One of us has to bring it to him, he can only play it while one of us is in the room, and we take it out of the cage when we leave the room."

"What if he won't give it back?" asked Nails

"We stop feeding him until he does."

We thought about it. Dread spoke up.

"Come on you guys. I just want to play music. If I bust up the guitar I know I won't ever get another one. Why would I do that?"

"There's another problem," said Nails. "What if he uses the guitar to hurt himself? Like uses the guitar strings to hang himself?"

That gave us pause.

"Well," said Bernadette, "it would solve our vigilante problem. None of us want to kill him, but if he does it himself . . . ."

"I can't believe this shit," said Dread. "I just want to play music."

We agreed to give it a try.

None of us knew anything about guitars so we brought up eBay on a laptop and let him pick out a bass guitar, along with a small amp and speaker. It arrived a couple days later and we set the amp up outside the bars and fed the guitar and cord in to him. Our only rule was that one of us had to be in the room. We also got some music videos and for him it was Christmas. He spent hours playing along with the videos. From what I could tell he wasn't bad but we hated the music.

We immediately bought the best noise-canceling headphones we could find so one of us could watch movies while he played. When he was done we'd have him slide the guitar out through the bars, make sure we had the cord, and stash everything far from the cell.

We tried to spend more time in the prison room. When we talked together we always did it where he could hear and enter into the conversation if he wanted. I got a deck of cards and we played Texas hold 'em for imaginary stakes.

At first he was suspicious.

"What's going on? You fuckers going to kill me with kindness? Well fuck you, I'm still in this fucking cell."

Saying nothing, we filed out the door and closed it.

A half hour later we came back as though nothing had happened and resumed. I tried to play catch through the bars, and that didn't work at all. When we got bored with that, Nails came over.

"Okay," he said, "show me a jab."

Dread assumed a boxer's pose and threw a left-handed jab, awkwardly.

"Holy crap. You say you actually won bar fights punching like that?"

"No," said Dread, "I usually had a pool cue or a beer bottle in my hand."

"You want to learn to box? Like a real fighter?"

"Sure."

"You ever going to hit a woman?"

"If she pisses me off."

WE LEFT. IMMEDIATELY. We stayed out an hour, then came back as though nothing had happened. Dread was confused.

"What the hell is this? Some kind of mind game? Well fuck you and your fucking games."

WE LEFT AGAIN. Came back again an hour and a half later. Nails walked up to the cage.

"You want to learn to box?"

"Yeah I want to learn."

"You ever going to hit a woman?"

"No man," he mumbled.

"No man what?"

"No man, I'll never hit a woman."

"I don't believe you, but at least it's the right answer. Okay, the stance. You right handed?"

"Yeah."

"Okay, left foot forward, pointing slightly right. Right foot back, that's it, only about forty-five degrees to the right. Knees bent, fists beside your head, like earmuffs, elbows down. That's it. Protected."

Nails worked on the stance, getting Dread into a good position.

"Right, now the jab. Slow motion. Watch me. You extend your left fist and turn it. Your arm turns, your shoulder turns, your fist ends up palm down. Okay, try it."

Dread tried it a few times.

"Remember, never let your elbow fly out. It's a weak punch when the elbow flies out. Turn the arm, turn the shoulder, straight line. When your shoulder turns it rises up to protect your chin. That's it."

"Okay, now stand with your left side next to the bars. Throw the jab and don't let your elbow hit those bars. For one thing, it'll hurt like hell. That's it. Straight. Palm down at the end. Slow motion. Get it right and then we'll add speed. Good. Jab . . . return . . . in your stance the elbows are down . . . jab . . . good. Okay, lesson over. But you can practice that any time you get bored. Technique first and then speed, right?"

Dread nodded. He kept practicing the jab.

"You ever going to hit a woman?"

"No."

"Good answer. I don't believe you, but it's the right answer."

# CHAPTER 31

WE BUILT THE new cell in the office next door to Dread's. The prisoners would never know it, because of the soundproofing, and it would be handy when it came to care and feeding. For Lucy, it was hard work, managing construction on the houseboat by day and working on the cell at night. We tried to take the load off, do as much of our construction as we could so she could grab some sleep. Also, we knew the drill now, having built the first cell together. We made some improvements. We took our time and in a month, it was done. Now all we had to do was find our next target.

Bernadette and I were in my office. I was curious.

"Is he still meditating?"

"Yeah. It's a competition. He wants to prove he can outdo me."

"So it's not like he's finding inner peace or anything like that."

"Oh hell no. He mumbles sometimes and I'm pretty sure they're swear words or words to old metal songs. We don't have a Buddha on our hands."

"I wonder if it matters. Just getting him to sit still for a couple of hours is a step in the right direction."

"Who knows?" she said. "He's a hard bastard, so I wouldn't count on it. He faked me out in the past, playing all nice and concerned and then bam! He'd start swinging."

"That's going to be a big problem," I said. "Even if he does change, how would we know? He's like a sociopath. He can fake anything."

"You said it. We won't have to worry about it now. He's not even pretending to change."

"That surprises me. Once he knows the plan you'd think he'd try to fake his way out."

"He's too angry and mean for that."

"And dumb."

"I'm not so sure," she said, "sometimes he surprises me."

# CHAPTER 32

THE NEWSPAPERS GAVE us our next target.

We were sitting around Dread's room eating takeout eggs Benedict a few mornings later and Bernadette brought in the *Seattle Times*. I know you can get the news online but I still subscribe. I love newspapers. On the front page was a familiar face. Eddie Moon had beaten another rap. Moon was known up and down the West Coast as a murderer, gangster, white slaver, drug kingpin and he had been finally caught.

Moon was brought to trial with an open-and-shut case and that very morning had beaten the rap. Dead witnesses, missing evidence and weak testimony. The front page of the paper had a full shot of him triumphant on the courthouse steps standing beside his lawyers with his arms raised in triumph.

"Okay," I said, "if we go, we might as well go big. What do you say?"

Everyone agreed he met all our criteria and everyone agreed it would be impossible to kidnap him. He had security up the yin-yang, he was known to be armed, and the police would be on his every move. How the hell could four amateurs with one lucky kidnapping hope to pull this off?

No one had an answer. Oddly, it was Nails who came up with a glimmer of an idea.

"There's no way we can get to him. But what if he came to us?"

"How," said Lucy.

"Hell if I know. I just thought of it. It worked with Dread."

"What do we have that he would want?" I asked.

"Hot chicks?" said Bernadette. "I hear he's a ladies' man."

"Think you and Lucy could pull it off?"

"Not a chance in hell."

"Okay, other ideas?"

"What does he want more than anything in the world?"

"I know," said Nails. "The head of that prosecutor who brought him to trial."

"Yeah, he'd love that. Do we have any prosecutor heads lying around?"

We were stumped.

That evening we went in again to keep Dread company. We'd been playing Texas Hold 'em and now we played for cash. Dread didn't have any so we gave him a thousand dollars in chips and the four of us had a game every night. We pulled the table over to the cell and Dread played through the bars. So far, he was down about $400, Nails and Lucy were winning and Bernadette and I were close to even.

Every night we played and Dread gradually joined in the conversations. He wasn't quite as dumb as we thought, possessing a cleverness that was surprising on occasion. On the other hand, he could barely read and had no concept of things like history and art. The rest of us talked about whatever we felt like and I had a slim hope that Dread was learning stuff from us. He had calmed down once he realized that every time he got angry or violent we just left the room. The longer he was in the cage the less he liked being alone.

# CHAPTER 33

BREAKFAST WITH DREAD had become a daily ritual. We'd give him a tray table and take it away when he was done. It was too easy to turn stuff like that into a weapon and we were resolved never to trust him. On the other hand, it didn't matter if he was in on our plans. If he got away we were doomed anyway because we'd already committed lots of crimes. Kidnapping, imprisonment, lying to the police. That made things easier because we didn't have to keep secrets from him. He already had enough to hang us all.

It was the morning after we'd read about Eddie Moon beating the murder charge. Apparently, his accountant had been caught doctoring the books. Who'd have thought? A criminal accountant committing a crime.

He was just about to flee the country when Eddie found out. He did not take it easily. The accountant's death was a grisly one and sadly for Eddie it took place in a warehouse the feds knew about. They'd hidden video cameras and one of them was perfectly placed. The tape had all the subtleties of The Texas Chainsaw Massacre. Open and shut, right?

Alas, the tape disappeared. It was a miracle! It also showed that Eddie's organization had tentacles into the police department, city hall and even the department of justice. Scary stuff. The prosecutor had promised to introduce the tape and was left holding an extremely weak case. Eddie walked.

"I would love to take this guy down," said Lucy, "but there's no way."

"You guys are batshit crazy," said Dread. "Not a chance in hell you could pull this off. You were lucky to get me, and I wasn't protected at all."

"Oh hell," said Nails, "you were just practice."

"You were lucky."

There was a pause there, because we all knew he might be right. That was amateur hour. This was the big leagues. It was time for me to drop my bombshell.

"We do have one advantage," I said.

"What's that?"

"I know him."

"No way," said Lucy, "you know Eddie Moon?"

"We're not pals, but I know him."

"What the hell," said Nails, "don't tell me you're mobbed up."

"No, nothing like that. But I'm rich, he's rich, sometimes we do rich people things. Country clubs, fancy restaurants, charity balls . . ."

"What would Eddie Moon be doing at a charity ball?" asked Lucy.

"Cover. He likes to pretend he's legit. People know he's not, but money can get you into a lot of places and some high society people think it's romantic to know a gangster. But after that trial he's the O.J. Simpson of Seattle. A pariah. Doors are closing all over town.

"Poor guy," said Bernadette. "Torture and kill one little accountant and all your friends turn on you."

"Yeah. He's dead meat," I said.

"How'd you meet him, Boss?" asked Nails.

"I was at the country club hitting some balls on the range

and Bill Bobbit asked if I wanted a game."

"Bill Bobbit? The chairman of Blaze?"

"Yeah."

"Wow, Boss, you do hang out with the big boys."

Blaze was a software company that had two video games go viral. Bobbit went from a basement hacker to a multimillionaire in about two years. Nice guy. Socially awkward and a terrible golfer.

"I said, 'sure', and it was only when I got out there that I realized Moon was one of the players. I wanted no part of him, but it was too late to back out so I played."

"Wow, I bet that was fun."

"No it wasn't. Moon had a friend with him and they challenged us to a team game for big stakes. Right away I knew something was up and I figured Eddie's friend was a ringer. We were being hustled."

"But weren't you a good golfer?" asked Nails.

"I was, but that was no help because Eddie knew it. I couldn't fake him out. You know anything about golf?"

"I've watched it on TV," said Nails.

"My brothers played," said Lucy, "so I know a little."

"Well, I needed an edge. Then I found it."

"What was that?"

"I'd played the club for years and knew the caddies. Never underestimate the value of friends in low places. I looked at the caddy on the hustler's bag and he gave me a slow wink. Right then I knew he would tip the match and he knew he was in for a slice of the winnings."

"Boss," said Nails, "you are a sly bastard."

"How'd it go?" asked Lucy.

"As you'd suppose. Those guys kept it close but by the time we got to the last hole there was big money on the table. Press bets, Vegas points, Comanche, KPs, side bets, Nostradamus— it was a large number."

"What the hell are you talking about?" asked Bernadette.

"Golf bets. You go to any course in the country and they've got bets you've never heard of."

"Comanche? Nostradamus?"

"It would take too long to explain, but trust me, they mounted up. We stood on the eighteenth tee and there was a lot of money riding on that hole. Moon said, 'Let's make it interesting. Double or nothing.'

"Bobbit was nervous, but I laughed and said, 'Hell, let's make it really interesting. We'll double your double or nothing.' Now we're into lots of money, even for rich people and Bobbit was sweating. Moon was excited. His partner, the hustler, might've caught a glimmer that something was up. But he couldn't back down now.

"'Done,' said Moon. 'Best ball, no strokes, one hole. Let's round it off, $90,000 apiece. Okay with you?'

"'Done,' I said. 'Bill, don't worry, I can cover you on this. I made the bet.' But Bobbit was game, I'll say that. He covered the bet."

"Oh boss," said Bernadette, "I don't know what the hell you're talking about but I'm still excited. What happened?"

"Well, I knew Moon and Bobbit were out of it unless one of them got lucky. Both were high handicappers and it was a long, uphill par four. Moon flew his tee shot out of bounds and threw his driver halfway down the fairway. He was done. The hustler stood up, took a brand-new swing, and laid it out there about 280, right down the middle. He looked at me with a little smirk and I laughed and said, 'Nice swing. Where you been hiding that one?'

"He laughed and said, 'Welcome to the big leagues.'

"It was Bobbit's turn and he took a mighty swing and caught about two dimples on the ball. Topped it thirty yards down the fairway. So it was up to the hustler and me.

"I'd been playing okay, nothing flashy, but it was money time. So I teed up my ball, took a little bigger shoulder turn and flushed one out there beside the hustler. His eyes got big. Game on.

"Moon hit a second ball, I have no idea why. He was lying three and no threat. We headed out with the caddies leading the way. Bobbit topped another one, so he was history and the hustler and I finally got to our two good tee shots.

"Our caddies were out in front of us, and wouldn't you know it? When we got to our balls that hustler's Titleist was lying right square in a divot. You talk about bad luck!

"Moon screamed for a free drop. They argued. They swore. But hey, golf is golf. You play it as it lies in a money game. I hit first and faded a nice 5-iron onto the green. Safe. The hustler did the best he could to dig his ball out of that divot but chunked it way short of the green. He hit a decent pitch shot, but missed his long par putt, and I two-putted for the win."

"Holy shit, Boss," said Bernadette, "I have no idea what the hell your talking about, but you made $90,000 on a golf match?"

"Yeah. So did Bobbit. But I didn't make that much. Later that night I gave the hustler's caddy twenty percent. Only he and I knew he'd nudged that ball into a divot and neither one of us was ever going to mouth off about scamming a killer."

"So Eddie hates your guts."

"Well, there is that. But I know him. I used to see him around the club but I doubt if they'd let him in now."

"Is there any way we can use that?" asked Lucy.

"I don't know. I do know he'd love to get back at me."

"Maybe that's it," she said.

"What?"

"Let him get back at you and catch him while he's doing it."

"At the golf course?"

"No. It has to be private. The best scenario would be to get him to come here alone, without anyone knowing. Some hush hush big money deal just between the two of you."

We thought about that and came up with nothing.

"Let's sleep on it," I said, "and meet in the morning."

# CHAPTER 34

I WOKE UP WITH a glimmer of an idea but I couldn't put it together. We met for breakfast next to Dread's cage and I asked if they had anything. They didn't.

"Here's all I can come up with," I said. "It can't be a legitimate deal. It has to be something shady where he thinks he can screw me. Ideally, he'd have something I want, but I can't think of anything. I'm trying to cut back on stuff. Live a little simpler."

They damn near fell down laughing.

"Boss, you own a building! In downtown Seattle! You drive a Mercedes S-class!"

"Yeah, but it's black. It's not like I'm flashing around in a Lamborghini."

"Whoo boy, you're damn near one of us normal people!"

They laughed again.

"Really. I've been trying to cut back."

This brought more laughter and I gave up.

"Come on, boss," said Nails, "he must have something you'd want."

Right then it came to me.

"What if we turn that around? What if I have something he wants? What if he thinks he can screw me out of it?"

"Do you have anything like that?" asked Bernadette.

I thought.

"I don't think so," I said, "but he doesn't know that."

I told them my idea and they felt it might have possibilities.

THE NEXT DAY, the four of us gathered.

"You sure you want to do this Boss?" asked Bernadette.

"Oh hell yes," I said.

"Do you think he'll go for it?"

"Who knows? I do know he hates me more now than ever. I'm in the inner circle and he's shut out. Also, he's dying to get back at me for the golf game and it's a shady deal where he could make out like a bandit. What's not to like?"

"Okay," said Nails. "Give it a shot."

I picked up the phone and dialed.

"Mr. Moon's office."

"Yes, may I speak to Eddie please. Tell him it's Monte Grant."

"Hold please."

He made me wait a couple of minutes.

"Grant?"

"Moon?"

"Yeah, this is Eddie and I'm still pissed off at you."

"Ah yes. That was sad, wasn't it?"

"You fucked me over. You know it and I know it."

"The way I remember it, you tried to fuck me over first. Right?"

"I didn't want you, I just wanted Bobbit. For that guy it was pocket change."

"Let's admit we tried to hustle each other and get on with this. I assume the feds are listening in?"

"Always."

"I bet you have a burner phone handy and I do too. Go

find a place that isn't wired and call me at this number. We'll talk."

Fifteen minutes later my burner phone rang.

"Okay," he said, "what's up?"

"I have a little cash flow problem."

"You want a loan. Go to a bank."

"That's part of the problem. I'm a bit sideways and if I go to a bank the story's going to come out. I can't have that."

"So you want to borrow from me?"

"No. I have something. It's worthless to me and could be big money for you. Way more than that golf bet."

"I don't trust you."

"I don't trust you either. That's a given."

"What have you got?"

"Did you know who my dad was?"

"A bit. Big Wall Street guy, right? Lost everything, got blown up trying to get to Grand Cayman?"

"That's him. Let's just say he was not pure of heart."

"He was a crook."

"That's a crude way of putting it. But true."

"What's he got to do with this?"

"You know he gave me this building? In the will?"

"Yeah."

"It's got a secret hiding place and I'm the only one who knew about it. He'd showed it to me years ago. When I got the building, I checked it out."

"And you found something."

"Right."

"What did you find?"

"A painting. A small one. And a note to me."

"What the fuck would I want with a painting?"

"It's not just any painting."

"I see. What is it?"

"A Goya. Do you know who that is?"

"Fuck you. I'm a gangster but I'm not illiterate. Everyone knows Goya. What did the note say?"

"It said not to sell the painting under any circumstances. Some European guy needed a big loan and gave my dad the painting as collateral. My dad knew it was suspicious. Okay, more than suspicious, he knew it was stolen. That painting's been missing for thirty years. If I show up with it I go straight to prison."

"I'd like that. See how you like prison you cheap bastard."

"You could turn me in," I said, "but they'd have to find the painting and I don't think they can. It's a really good hiding place. But there's another possibility."

"What?"

"I know there are art collectors out there who don't care about legal technicalities and they'd pay a fortune for this."

"Perfect. Find one and sell it to him."

"Nope. I have no connections to that world. Also, there are agents out there posing as collectors. I have no chance of sorting out who's real and who's Interpol or FBI."

"I see. So you need someone."

"I need someone with connections."

"What do I get out of it?"

"You get to buy low and sell high. Very high. I need money in a hurry. Are you interested?"

"I might be. What if I pay you and find out the Goya is a fake?"

"I assume you'd kill me. It would be really stupid on my part."

"True. Let me check around and get back to you. What's the name of the painting and how much do you want?"

I told him.

# CHAPTER 35

"WHAT DO YOU think?" I asked.

"I think he bought it," said Bernadette. "It sounds foolproof. How do we capture him?"

"I've got a cunning plan."

"No shit, Boss," said Lucy. "You're a Black Adder fan?"

"Absolutely. Love that show. You too?"

"Oh hell yes. Best British show ever."

"You guys done talking TV?" asked Nails. "Don't we have better things to discus?"

"Right," I said, "How are you guys with electronics?"

They stared at me blankly. Oops. A flaw in my plan. Then Bernadette spoke up.

"Lucy knows some, but our best bet is Dread. He works sound and lights for the band, he knows all that stuff."

"I don't trust him," said Nails. "No way we put this in his hands."

"We can double check his work," I said, "if he can do what we need."

We went over to the prison room and I laid out my plan to Dread.

"Is that possible?" I asked.

"Oh hell yes. You've already got the taser. But what do I get out of it?"

"What do you want?"

"Freedom."

"No chance. Think of something else."

"I want a bigger amp and speaker. I want to rock out and I want my bass in here all the time so I can play whenever I feel like it."

We talked about that. Could he bend the bars with it? Could he jab us? We tried to think of every possibility and couldn't come up with a reason for him not to have it.

"Okay," I said. "Lucy, will the soundproofing hold up?"

"It should. We can always go outside the room and listen but I put in the heaviest stuff available."

"Okay Dread, you got it."

"When do we start?"

"Soon. We're waiting for a phone call."

"Boss," said Bernadette, "we got a problem."

"What's that?"

"Our plan is to give Moon video access to the building, right? So he can check to see you're not up to anything?"

"Right."

"We can't show him all the rooms in the building. He'll see Dread in prison and the other room with the cage."

"Damn. I didn't think of that."

I looked at the others.

"Any ideas?"

"Sure, it's easy," said Lucy. "We put fake pictures up of two empty offices. Everything else in the building is legit, he'll see people walking around, business as usual. Two offices empty. If he asks, just tell the truth about the phone center that moved to India. Then when he comes at night we just turn off the lights in the prison rooms. It makes sense."

We thought about it. It should work.

EDDIE MOON CALLED THE NEXT NIGHT.

"You alone?" he asked.

"Yeah," I said.

"Call this number."

I called back on a burner phone.

"I can't pay that much," he said.

I knew he'd try to screw me. I'd have been suspicious if he didn't.

"You're going to make out like a bandit. We both know that. Don't fuck around."

"Hey," he said, "I had to try. Okay, you got a deal."

"You got that kind of money?"

"I wouldn't be talking if I didn't. When do I come?" he asked.

"Thursday. Two a.m.. All the offices are empty and the cleaning crew is done by then. You can check to make sure everyone leaves the building but me. Remember, alone. No weapons. Park a couple blocks away and walk. I don't want your car near my building."

"Got it. How do I check the building."

"You got an iPad?"

"Probably. If not I can get one."

"Here's the website for all the cameras in the building. You can scan now and make sure all the rooms are covered. I'll meet you in the lobby. We'll do a metal detector and X-ray over by the elevators, out of sight of the front windows. Make sure we're both unarmed."

"You don't trust me?"

"You're joking, right? After we know we're both unarmed we head up to my office, have a couple of drinks and do the deal."

"Okay. See you then."

THE EQUIPMENT WE NEEDED was already in the building and Lucy had bought the electronics Dread asked for. That night we hauled the device onto the freight elevator and manhandled it into the prison room.

"You'll have to let me out to work on that thing," said Dread.

"Nope. Not going to happen. You do it through the bars and we'll help out here. One bad move and the deal's off."

He grudgingly agreed and that night we took turns handing him tools through the bars, one at a time, making sure they came back out before the next one went in. The tools were small, so he couldn't do much damage even if he wanted to.

He did the installation and we hauled the machine back downstairs.

# CHAPTER 36

BY THURSDAY NIGHT everything was in place. Nails and Lucy were circling the streets in the Toyota, watching to see if Eddie had reneged on his word and brought backup. They too had an iPad so they could make sure none of Eddie's goons tried to sneak in. We made Bernadette take the kids to a hotel nearby. If anything went wrong, we wanted her to be able to run for it.

By two a.m., Nails and Lucy had checked in with an all-clear and I took the elevator down to the lobby. Precisely on time, Eddie drove up and parked a couple of blocks away. He was alone, carrying the iPad. He sat in the car and checked the cameras. I was the only person in the building. He got out of his car, still checking the iPad, and walked to the front door. I let him in.

"Eddie," I said.

"Monte," he replied, "no weapons?"

"You can pat me down if you want, but the metal detector and X-ray are over there, out of sight. I think they're safer."

"Okay, lead the way."

I walked over and switched them on.

"You go first," he said, and I did. I passed through the metal detector. No beeps.

"Okay?" I asked.

"Come over here."

I did, and he patted me down. I was clean.

"Those are your machines. I don't trust them. I like old fashioned methods."

"I understand. No problem. Your turn."

He stepped through the metal detector. No beeps.

I walked to the X-Ray machine and stepped in. He checked the screen. No plastic Glock pistol, no ceramic knives. I stepped out and he stepped in.

And . . . nothing.

Oops.

What the hell!!!

Dread had promised the second guy through the X-Ray machine would get tased. The plan was to tase Eddie, tie him up, and congratulate ourselves on a masterful kidnapping. Damn! It'd been such a good plan. What the hell had gone wrong? Had Dread double crossed us? I was doomed.

What would Sam Spade do? What would Spenser do? Easy, they'd level Eddie with one punch. Problem solved. Me? I'd never leveled anyone with a punch in my life. I went into stall mode. Okay, maybe "panic mode" was a better term. This was going to get very tricky and all I could think of was to lead Eddie over to the elevators and take him up to the office.

We took the elevator up and I hoped he didn't see me shaking in fear. I let him into my office. I'd set out a bottle of Champagne to celebrate the kidnapping, so all I could think of was to open it and pour a glass for Eddie and me.

"A toast," I said, "to Goya."

"Right. Don't you have anything stronger?"

"I could run upstairs and get some scotch or bourbon."

"Naw, too much work, and I want to see the painting."

That was a problem. I didn't have a painting, much less a

Goya. Bernadette and I had done a search of stolen paintings that were still missing and the Goya was one of them. It was small, it was worth five or six million, and nobody had seen it for thirty years. Perfect.

Damn, damn, damn.

"Okay," I said, "let me get it. It's hidden because we weren't sure you'd come alone."

"You don't trust me?"

We both laughed.

Just then the door opened behind him and Nails softly stepped in. Never, ever have I been so happy to see anyone in my life. But Eddie heard the door and spun around. Nails caught him with two quick jabs and a right cross. I waited for Eddie to fall. Instead he laughed. Oops again.

Nails was a middleweight; Eddie was thirty pounds heavier and could take a punch. Couldn't anything go right? Nails circled and Eddie closed in for the kill. I looked for a weapon of any kind. Can you knock someone out with a stapler? Probably not. Eddie now had his back to the door and that's when two arms reached in swinging an iPad. Lucy was a strong woman and she caught him on the back of the head. It put Eddie down. We all jumped on him and punched until he stopped moving. Then we searched for something to tie him up. Oops again. The duct tape was downstairs, perfectly placed for an X-Ray machine taser victim.

I raced around like an idiot, looking for another roll while Nails calmly took off his belt and wrapped up Eddie's wrists. Lucy, seeing this, slipped her leather belt out of her jeans and did the same with his feet.

It was then I found the extra duct tape.

We slapped some on for extra security and dragged Eddie to the elevator. We took him down one floor, dragged him out and into his prison room. We finally, gratefully, got him inside and locked the lock. Only then did we cut off the duct tape and take back the belts. I went over and flopped into a chair.

"I can't tell you how happy I am you guys showed up," I said. "How'd you know?"

"We were watching our iPad," said Lucy. "We saw you go through the machine, then him, and nothing happened. We thought oh shit, Monte is screwed. So we rushed back to the building and came up the freight elevator. Good work on stalling him till we got there."

"I'm just glad I didn't pee my pants. Let's go drink that Champagne," I said.

"Aren't you forgetting something?" said Lucy.

"Oh shit. The car."

It wouldn't do to have Eddie's car found a couple blocks away from our building. He'd been wearing dark clothes and so was I. He was bigger than me, but that couldn't be helped, so I was chosen to get rid of the car. I took the elevator back downstairs, left through the front door, and walked in the direction he'd come from. There weren't a lot of cars and I clicked his electric key in my pocket until one lit up. Keeping my head down I got in, started it up and drove south of town to the industrial area. I looked back and Lucy was following me in the Toyota. I found a deserted spot behind some abandoned warehouses, stopped and got out. We'd watched CSI and we knew the drill. She parked a few car lengths away, opened her trunk and got out a two-gallon container of gasoline. We poured it all over his car, threw the container inside and lit it. Then we got the hell out of there.

Oh sure, there would be tire tracks, but there must be thousands of Toyota Camrys in the Northwest. Not to worry. Footprints? We both wore Birkenstocks, the uniform shoes of Seattle, and threw them away on the way back.

Nails was waiting for us in the basement when we drove in.

"Finished?" he asked.

"Yeah, and I'm beat," I said. "Have we forgotten anything?"

"What the hell happened with that taser?"

"I don't know. I walked through the X-Ray first, just as we planned. Then Eddie walked through, and nothing happened."

"Let's go take a look," said Lucy. "I could've sworn Dread had that thing all set up."

We went up to the lobby and over to the machine. Lucy took off her jacket and waved it through the machine. It got tased. Damn.

Oh well, if we ever wanted to kidnap a jacket we now had the equipment.

# CHAPTER 37

I'D SET THE ALARM for 7:00 a.m. I got a screwdriver out of Lucy's toolbox and went down to the lobby to take the taser and electronics out of the X-Ray machine. Dread had showed me how and when it was back to normal I headed upstairs. I cleaned up and went down to my office. Bernadette and the kids were back, coffee was on, and we grabbed some before we went to check on our new prisoner. He started yelling as soon as we entered the room and flicked on the lights.

"What the fuck is this? You people are fucking dead! I will cut you up, I will make you beg me to kill you . . . ."

He went on like that for awhile while we sat quietly and watched. It was impressive, but eventually he ran out of threats and just stood there gripping the bars so hard the veins stood out on his forehead. In a calmer, deadlier voice, he said, "Monte, what the fuck is going on?"

"You've been kidnapped," I said.

"Are you fucking insane? You think you'll get ransom? Even if you do, there's no place you can hide. Nowhere in the world. We will find you!"

"No, it's not a ransom thing." I said. "We just want you off the streets. Think of it as a public service."

"You are insane! That's the craziest thing I ever heard of."

"Yeah, you're probably right. We all thought it was crazy too. Then it kind of grew on us."

"I can't fucking believe this. How do you think it's going to work out? My guys are going to find you. They're going to kill you. I'll be out of here so fast it'll make your head spin."

"First of all, how are they going to find us? Did you tell anyone where you were going?"

He paused. I could practically hear him thinking.

"Maybe."

"Nope. I don't think so. You see what I did there? I bet my life on you not telling anyone because you'd want all the money for yourself."

"You better hope so, or you're dead."

"They would've been here by now. Here, you want to check the computer and see all the people coming to rescue you? Oh look! Just normal people coming to work. No goons rushing in with guns. Face it, nobody knows you're here," I continued, "you are, in fact, gone. Vanished. Without a trace."

Eddie screamed and yelled, threatened, and we sat and watched. It was a pretty good show. He wound down, and then thought.

"You dumb fucks. The only way you can make money is to try for ransom and nobody's going to pay. You did all this for nothing!"

"You're right. Except that we've taken you out of action. That's all we wanted, because the world will be better without you."

"You haven't changed a thing. Nothing. The organization will keep doing the same things it always has. Drugs will come in, protection rackets will stay the same, all that stuff. You haven't changed a fucking thing."

"We know. All we did was take you out of the picture. Correct an injustice. You should've gone to prison and now you have. Hooray for our side."

"So what now? You keep me in this cell? Forever?"

"I guess so, unless you convince us it's a lot less work just to kill you and dispose of the body. At the moment, I'd bet we're leaning in that direction. We'll give you a month or two and maybe take a vote. Or maybe not. Our plans aren't very firm at this point."

"This is the craziest fucking thing I've ever heard of. Are you guys some kind of cult? Are you the Manson Family?"

"No, not a cult, but I guess we would qualify as crazy. We can live with that. Sweet dreams."

We got up and walked out. Eddie was still yelling when we turned out the lights and shut the door.

# CHAPTER 38

WE MET THE NEXT morning in Dread's room. He was looking forward to his new amp and speakers and we'd brought him quiche for breakfast. I'm not sure he knew what it was, but he wolfed it down.

"It must've worked, right?" asked Dread, from inside his cell.

"Like a charm," I said.

We'd agreed not to tell him about the glitch. What purpose would it serve?

"Good work on the taser," I said, "I had a terrible fear it would go off when I went in, but it didn't. How'd you do that?"

"Simple. I just set it up to trigger on the second guy through, like you told me."

Was it possible Dread couldn't count to two? It didn't matter. Electronics are tricky and we'd captured our guy.

"Well, we have another prisoner, and Eddie Moon makes you look like Peter Pan."

"I've heard lots of stories," said Dread. "He is a seriously evil dude. You guys really are crazy."

"Yeah, I guess we are."

"How long are you going to keep him locked up?"

"Who knows? We figure you've got a chance of turning yourself around. Him? We could be talking two or three lifetimes."

Dread looked around at the four of us.

"You guys in this for the long haul?"

"Sure," said Nails. "It's not like we have to give up our lives or anything. We can go do what we want. You guys aren't going anywhere. And Monte's building has become our home. It's like I've got a new family."

"Me too," said Bernadette. "And I have free babysitters. How cool is that?"

"I'd like to talk," said Lucy, "but I've got to go to work. I'll see you all tonight."

"We better check him out," said Nails. "You know he's going to be trouble. I'd say the odds of him turning into a good person are about eight billion to one."

"That good?" laughed Bernadette.

Bernadette, Lucy and I trooped over to Moon's prison room and turned on the lights. He was still sleeping, or faking it."

"Wakey wakey," said Nails. "Welcome to the first day of the rest of your life."

Eddie rolled over on his mat and glared at us.

"I thought it was a bad dream," he said. "A dream about some crazy fuckers with a death wish."

"Nope," I said, "this is real. You want some water?"

"I want coffee. And a gun. I want to see you all bleeding on the floor."

We got up and walked out. The training, no matter how futile, had begun.

TWO DAYS LATER the news broke.

The front page of the *Seattle Times* had it first but then it spread to national news. Eddie Moon, the notorious murderer who'd slimed his way out of a guilty verdict, was missing. Police all over the Northwest were questioning suspects, the Feds were conducting investigations, and the general consensus was that either his own gang or a rival gang had put him in a shallow grave. They'd found his car where Nails had ditched it, torched to a blackened hulk with no body inside.

Every day we moved back and forth from cell to cell. Maybe we were getting used to Dread, or maybe he was playing us, but he seemed like a better guy. Then again, he might've just looked better in comparison to Eddie, who was evil incarnate. Dread was a bozo, Eddie had risen to the top in a cutthroat world. He was wildly intelligent and far more deadly. He didn't bother with threats, or mindless yelling. He observed us as much as we observed him. One day we were outside his cell drinking coffee and talking about our plans. It didn't matter what he heard or saw. If he ever got out we were all dead no matter what he knew.

"Lucy," Nails said, "your plan worked but we've got to figure some sort of end game. Eddie here is never going to change. Do we keep him forever? Are we talking life in prison?"

"I don't know," said Lucy, "I just figured every day he was out of circulation would be a win for humanity. We've probably saved lives already because he's such a psychopath. He likes to kill people. Right, Eddie?"

"She's got a point," said Eddie. "I don't give a shit, it's the law of the jungle."

"Well, think of this as a new jungle," said Nails.

"You guys don't know how this is going to end, do you?" said Eddie.

"No, Eddie, we don't," I said. "Do you?"

"Of course I do. It's simple. One of you is going to break. One of you won't be able to take the strain and you're going to rat out the others. That's the way it works."

"You haven't thought this through," I said. "If one of us breaks, what would they do?"

"Go to the Feds, try to get their life back."

"Nope," I said. "We're all free now. We can do what we want. If any of us cops out it means we either all go to prison or your guys kill us."

"Bet your ass they would. You kidnap me, you pay the price."

"So why would we rat the others out?"

"I could buy you off. Pay one of you big bucks to set me free."

"Yeah, that'd be a good deal. Again, they'd be dead the moment you got out."

"Trust me. There's a Judas among you. They'll find a way."

"Trust us. We knew that possibility going in. We've talked about it for over a year and we haven't come up with a way one of us could gain anything by giving up the others."

"I could promise immunity. Set me free and I'll protect you."

We laughed.

"Yeah," I said, "that'll work. We'd stand a better chance trusting North Korea."

"All I know is nothing's perfect. You guys have slipped up somewhere and it's going to bite you in the ass."

"I've thought about that," said Nails, "and even if it happens it's worth a shot. I love seeing you in that cage and I love the thought that we put you there. This is way better than going to the zoo."

"You think I'm some sort of animal?"

"No, if you were an animal I'd want to set you free. With you, I wish we'd made the cage smaller."

# CHAPTER 39

THE POLICE CAME again the next day. By now Bernadette and the kids had moved up into my penthouse. My office was back to looking like a business, with her at the front desk when she wasn't watching the kids. She was there when they walked in.

"Can I help you?" she said.

They were two new detectives in slacks, sport coats that had seen better days and shirts and ties. They looked tired. They showed her their badges and asked to speak to both of us. She ushered them into my office. I pushed a button under the desk that recorded the interview. Police have video cameras everywhere, I figured turnabout was fair play. Mine was hidden in a modern bronze sculpture of an old camera on a tripod. Obvious. But no one had ever tumbled.

"Mr. Grant," said the older of the two, a black man with gray in his hair and a weary look on his face. "You're a private detective, right?"

"Yes."

"How long have you been in business?"

"About four years."

"Do you have many clients?"

"No."

"So you're a failure?"

"I guess, but now and then something comes along and it occupies my time."

"How do you make money? How do you afford this office?"

"This is kind of embarrassing," I said, "but I own the building. Also I have a trust fund."

"So you're rich."

"I guess you could say that, but I still like being a detective."

"What kind of crimes do you work?"

"Mostly white-collar stuff. I do know money and I'm pretty good at figuring out when it's not adding up right."

"Why do you need a secretary if business is so poor?"

"I don't. But now and then someone comes in and also I need help with the paperwork. Mostly her job is to take care of that."

"Okay. And where is your home?"

"It's one floor up. When I found my dad had left me the building I reserved the penthouse for myself."

"You live alone?"

"I have a friend staying with me at the moment, and Bernadette lives there too."

"I see. Are you a couple?"

"No. Just friends. She has two small children and this arrangement is easier for both of us."

"Don't the children bother you?"

"Not at all. We have lots of rooms and she and the kids have their own space. Is this relevant to your investigation?"

"Why do you think we're conducting an investigation?"

"I can't think of any other reason for you to be here. I'm sorry, was this a social call?"

"No, it's an investigation. Do you remember where you were last Thursday night?"

"Yes. I was upstairs in my home."

"How do you know?"

"Because that's where I am every night. I'm sixty, I'm quiet, I don't go clubbing."

"You don't visit friends, or have them visit you?"

"Well, Bernadette is with me always and at the moment I have another friend staying with me. As I say, it's a big place."

"So they can both vouch for you being home that night?"

I looked at Bernadette.

"Bernadette, were we all home last Thursday night?"

"Yes Boss."

"Okay," I said, "they'll vouch for me. What's all this about?"

"Our traffic cameras picked up a car that may have been involved in a crime. It was parked two blocks from here."

"I see," I said.

"It parked there at 2:00 a.m. and drove away shortly thereafter."

"Okay. Did your cameras pick up who was in the car?"

"I should probably ask the questions. That's the way we like to do it."

"Okay."

"Did anyone visit you that night? Other than the people who are staying in your apartment?"

"No. No one visited."

Bernadette looked a bit concerned. Luckily the detectives were staring at me.

"Do you have any idea why anyone would visit the building at that hour?"

"Well, we have fifteen floors of offices here. That person might've visited any one of them. Maybe they forgot something and came back to get it."

"We don't think the owner of the car worked here."

"That's odd," I said.

"So you have no idea why that person would park down the street at 2:00 a.m. come in to this building, go back out and drive off?"

Holy shit. They had video of Moon coming into my building. But the video couldn't be that good because when I went out to get rid of the car, they thought that was Moon too. Traffic cameras are high up, we were both wearing dark clothes, so it made sense. From above, on a dark night, could they tell?

"I have no idea," I said. "Who is this guy? Why is he so important?"

"We'll get to that later."

He turned to Bernadette.

"Do you remember anything from that night?"

"No sir," she said. "The kids go to bed early and I'm usually worn out so I just watch TV for awhile and go to sleep. It was like any other night."

"Okay," said the detective. The other one hadn't said a word during the whole interview. He was smaller, white, and didn't look like a cop at all. He had wispy brown hair and wore glasses. He looked like a science teacher.

"You got anything you want to ask, Ed?"

The little guy thought for a second.

"You didn't happen to look down and see the car, did you?" he asked.

"No. It's a long way down. I doubt if I would've noticed."

"Right."

And that was it. But it was worrying. I called Nails in the penthouse and told him.

"They spotted the car?" he said.

"Yeah, and the traffic cameras caught Eddie coming in and me going out. I don't think they knew it was two different people but you know they're going to study that video.

# CHAPTER 40

THAT NIGHT WE gathered in Dread's room. We filled in Lucy and Dread and then tried to figure what to do next.

"You know the big problem?" said Lucy.

"What?"

"They might want to search the building."

"Damn," said Nails. "We can't keep these offices locked. How do we keep the cops out?"

"Uh oh," said Dread. "You master planners have fucked up. I might be getting out soon."

"That's right," I said. "We have to deal with this."

"Let me think," said Lucy. "We can't keep them out of the offices . . . ."

We sat quietly, thinking.

"We're on the fourteenth floor, right?"

"Right."

"Is there a thirteenth floor?"

"No. Most buildings don't have a thirteenth floor. Well they do, but they call it the fourteenth."

"And are there any occupied offices on this floor?"

"No. They knocked out walls to make the big phone rooms. It was the only company on this floor."

"So what if we make the floor disappear?"

"The entire floor???"

"The cops will use the elevators, right? No way they're going to climb up fourteen flights of stairs."

"Right."

"So we have to get the elevators to skip this floor. Go right from twelve to fifteen."

"But the office number will be wrong. The elevators will say fifteenth floor and my office number is 1501."

"Easy to change that. No one from below ever comes up there, do they?"

"No. Except Willie with the mail."

"Can you go down for the mail early, tell him you're expecting something?'

"Sure, that'll work."

"We could rig the elevators just for the time the police are here. Make the floor disappear."

"The good news is it's just my office on the fifteenth floor. We just have to change that number. That shouldn't be hard.

"The elevator thing seems complicated," I said. "There has to be an easier way."

"I can't think of anything," said Nails, "can you guys?"

They shook their heads.

"Dread? Any ideas?"

"Yeah. I've got a good one. I want them to find me!"

"Ah, right. Maybe you're not the guy to ask."

"Maybe," said Bernadette, "you don't have to rewire the elevators. You just have to change the buttons. Put a fake panel over the real one that eliminates this floor."

It was a thought, and a good one. Lucy went out to check the panels on the elevators.

"There's one more huge problem," said Bernadette. "How do we know when they're coming?"

Damn.

# CHAPTER 41

WE COULDN'T FIGURE out Dread. It had gotten to the point where we felt comfortable around him. When he wanted, he could be engaging to talk to. Our breakfasts and dinners with him had become a ritual. We forced ourselves to have lunch with Eddie, but he projected evil vibes. The kicker with Dread was that we still didn't trust him. He'd figured out that it didn't pay to go against us, to be pissed off all the time, but we didn't trust the new Dread. We talked about it. We talked about it with him in the room. Why not? He and Eddie knew everything anyway. We wanted them either out of circulation forever or totally changed human beings. With Eddie, the second was like hoping to find a unicorn inside a wolverine.

So we ate breakfast and talked. Sometimes Nails stayed with Dread after breakfast. Bonding. A homeless guy and a guy in a cage.

"Dread," said Nails, "you're faking this nice guy thing pretty well. I'm proud of you."

"How do you know I'm faking?"

"Because at heart you're an asshole and you and I know it. You beat up Bernadette for Christ's sake. Only a raving jerk would ever do that."

"You're right," said Dread. "I can see that now."

"Bullshit. If we let you out today you'd be beating up some defenseless bastard tomorrow. You ever beat up homeless people?"

"No."

"I don't believe that either."

"You're never going to believe me, so this is never going to end, is it?"

"Not if I get a vote," said Nails. "But at least you're trying to fake being a good guy. I like that better than the screamer you used to be."

"I owe it all to you, Nails. You taught me how to fake being a good guy. And you know something? You fake it too. You're a fucking fraud."

"How do you figure?"

"That whole wino thing you do? I know winos and you're not one of them. No one goes on binges and then sobers up. That's bullshit."

"Maybe I'm overdoing the sobering up part."

"Either that or you're faking the binges."

"You got that wrong. If you ever get out of here I'll take you on one. You think you're a big-time drinker-doper guy but you're just a rookie. It would've taken you another two or three years to hit rock bottom."

"You think I'd hit rock bottom?"

"I think you could've been a world class meth head if you'd kept going. There was no upside to your life."

"Oh shit. I'm being analyzed by a homeless guy! Okay, Dr. Phil, tell me about my life."

"Easy. Your band sucks, or you wouldn't be playing biker bars and dives. I'm guessing you're some sort of grunge heavy metal band and you're about thirty years out of date hoping the music will make a comeback. Fat chance. So you've got a dead end gig, the only way you get chicks is with drugs, and you drive around in a crappy van you share with two other guys. I don't call that the fast track to stardom."

"Every band starts like that. That's why they're called garage bands."

"How often did you practice?"

"Two, three times a week."

"That's not practice. That's amateur shit."

"Fuck you. I played every day. Just not always with the band."

"How many hours?"

"I'd play an hour or two."

"Fuck me. An hour or two? When I was boxing I'd do six, seven hours a day. Jump rope, weights, running, working the bags, sparring. An hour or two. I'm surprised you made it to biker bars."

"I had other things to do."

"Yeah. You had your drug business to run. You had to boss around your woman. You had to play video games. Right?"

"Hey. I did the best I could."

"Are you shitting me? That was the best you could? What a pussy!"

"You're starting to piss me off, Dr. Phil."

"What are you going to do? Beat me up? Did you forget? I'm not a woman."

"I could kick your ass."

"Dream on. Maybe some day, after you've trained seven hours a day for five or six years, you might cause me a little trouble. Face it, you suck as a bass player and you suck even more as a fighter."

"So what's your plan? You going to change me by beating me down every day? Hell, my dad took care of that years ago."

"Oh no! You had a rough childhood? I never heard that before. Oh wait. Every boxer I ever knew had a rough childhood. Most of them took up boxing so they could go back and beat up their dads or stepdads."

"You ever wanted beat up your dad?"

"Nope. I had a good dad and a good mom. I just liked boxing. Against guys. Too bad they don't let guys fight women. You could've been a champ."

"Fuck you! I know it's wrong to beat up women."

"No you don't, or you wouldn't have done it."

"She made me do it. She pushed me too far."

"Oh yes! The cry of the wife beater! She made me do it! Are you that fucking stupid?"

"She was on me all the time. Get a job! Do something!"

"Wow! What an evil bitch! She wanted you to have a better life. She deserved what she got."

"It wasn't like that."

"It was exactly like that. You're an idiot."

"Fuck you."

"I'm going to work out now. Try not to cry about your rough childhood, it might distract me."

"Fuck you."

Nails laughed and jumped rope awhile. Then he went over to the heavy bag.

He punched a long time and when he finally dropped his hands he was wringing wet, exhausted. He crumpled to the floor and sat there. Done. Then he looked up.

"That's how you deal with hard times my friend. When you get knocked down you get up and deal with it again. Over and over, and that's what life is. Deal with it. Man the fuck up."

He slowly got to his feet and staggered out of the room.

# CHAPTER 42

LUCY WAS IN the other room alone with Eddie. It was late at night. She had a snifter of brandy and just sat there, looking at him.

"What do you want," he sneered.

"Nothing. I just want to see what you look like."

"Well take a good look, sister. Because someday I'm going to be your worst nightmare."

"Wow. I've only heard that line in ten or fifteen movies. Way to be original."

"Who the fuck are you?"

"I'm the one who came up with this plan."

"You planned to kidnap me?"

"Not you, just some awful person. I had some extra money and thought I could send food to Africa or I could take some evil person out of circulation. I chose the evil person option."

"No shit! This is like a school project?"

Lucy laughed.

"Yeah, I guess you could say that. I figured if I took a really bad guy off the streets I could save a lot of lives."

"Well that's just fucking stupid. Crime doesn't stop because I'm gone. Someone else will step up and it'll be just the same."

"I don't know. From what I heard, you were the worst of the worst. You are a psychopath, right?"

"Who knows? I do what I have to do."

"Oh bullshit. You love what you do. You love blood and pain and killing. You're a nut job."

It was Eddie's turn to laugh.

"You don't get it, do you? You can't keep me in here forever and when I get out you will die a long, slow, painful death. I guarantee it."

"Worst nightmare . . . long, painful death . . . I feel like I'm in a Clint Eastwood movie. You gotta work on your lines."

"Fuck you. Before I kill you I'm going to fuck you. And after I kill you, I'm going to fuck you again."

"Better! That's real psychopath shit. Now I know we got the right guy."

"Who the fuck are you?"

"I'm Lucy. I'm your worst nightmare," she laughed.

"What, 'cause you got me in a cage? Whoo, like I never been there before."

"I know. You did time."

"I did time in places that make this look like the fucking Hilton."

"And there were bigger guys there, right? Monsters?"

"Hell yes, but I made it. I made it by being the craziest motherfucker who ever lived."

"Oh good! I was hoping we didn't end up with the second or third craziest motherfucker. That would've been disappointing."

"So what's the plan, bitch? You going to kill me? As I see it, you got no other option."

"That is a possibility. The other one is that we just keep you here. Like a pet tiger. People pay to see dangerous animals in cages, so we could charge big bucks for you."

"Very fucking funny."

"Yeah, I am sometimes. As I see it, this is my private zoo. And you're the tiger. You can think of me and my friends as your keepers."

"I'll get you all you fucks."

"What you should worry about is what if something happens to us? What if we have an accident or something and no one in the world knows about this room and this cage? That would be what you would call a slow, painful death."

"I'll see you all in hell."

"Maybe, as you're dying, all your victims could come to you in your dreams, like the ghosts of Christmas past. You know that story? Tiny Tim?"

"I don't know what the hell you are talking about."

"We've got loads of time. Maybe I'll find the video. I'd find the book but I don't picture you as a reader. Can you read?"

"Fuck you. I can read, I know money, I run an organization. I'll squash you."

"Like a bug. You're supposed to say, "I'll squash you like a bug. You got to work on your clichés."

"Fuck you."

"Fuck you, Lucy. Try to be polite," Lucy laughed. "And just remember, putting you here was my idea. All mine."

"I won't forget. You are dead."

Lucy got up and walked to the door.

"I think," she said, "I may have the world's first psychopath zoo. I wonder if Netflix wants to do the documentary."

She turned and walked out.

# CHAPTER 43

DREAD'S BAND MATES had not given up, but they were slowing down. Prowling the city had only resulted in the one sighting of Bernadette and that had been a fiasco. She'd ditched them, and they hadn't seen her since because she no longer walked downtown. She drove the Toyota Camry with dark, tinted windows and she shopped far from our building. Just in case, Nails always went with her.

Bernadette drove them up out of the basement garage and headed across the floating bridge to Bellevue. She loved Bellevue because it was the opposite of her old life with Dread. It was upscale, filled with executives from Microsoft and Boeing and posh women who spent their days in high-end stores. Once I found out she loved it, I financed the excursions to her favorite mall, Bellevue Square. I got her a company credit card and told her to buy some clothes that fit in. I had her buy clothes for Nails too. So now, maybe once a week they headed over the floating bridge to Bellevue for shopping, lunch, toddler stuff, and whatever else we needed.

She drove to the mall and parked. She looked nothing like the woman who'd ridden Harleys. Dressed stylishly, wearing sunglasses, she led Nails into the mall. Nails had on his mall clothes—chinos and a sports shirt. They separated when they got inside and put their phones on speed dial just in case. Then Bernadette went off to shop and Nails wandered aimlessly, stopping for a Dairy Queen cone. He sat on a bench and ate it slowly. He saw a wine shop and realized he hadn't had a drink in three weeks. Somehow the craving wasn't as strong as it used to be and he felt guilty. Was he no longer mourning his wife and child? That was what always triggered his binges, but lately he'd been too busy to dwell on the past. He realized he was enjoying being with Monte, Bernadette and Lucy. He was enjoying doing crazy stuff. He was spending more time in the penthouse and less on the streets.

DEX AND EARL, Dread's band mates, were feeling heat. Always before they'd gotten their drugs in south Seattle and they knew the bar scene there. They knew who was to be trusted and they knew where to get product. But their main guy had been arrested two weeks ago and they were afraid he might talk, so Dex and Earl were forced to develop new sources. Believe it or not, there was a biker bar in Bellevue. It wasn't one of the big, blowout bars they were used to, but it was good enough. It was a cinder block building out by an industrial park in the low end of Bellevue, which would've been pretty mid range in any other city. The police knew the bar and left it alone as long as there were no fights and few complaints.

Dex and Earl had heard about it and checked it out. It was too quiet for their tastes, but you could drink and talk to Harley guys. They knew sooner or later they could score some product and it would be safer.

They shot pool and drank beer for a couple of hours, playing with whoever put their quarters on the table. They talked to guys but they were new in town. Narcs were known to ride choppers and look the part, so the conversations were guarded until a couple guys walked in and ordered beer. Typical. Boots, jeans, Harley tee shirts and obviously regulars. They came back to the pool table and put quarters on the rail. Then one of them looked closely and said, "Hey, I know you guys. You're in a band, right?"

Dex and Earl brightened up.

"Yeah," said Dex. "We play the bars."

"Hell yes. You guys are so fucking loud! And you got a singer, right? I saw him bust a heckler with a beer bottle. Laid him out!"

"Yeah, that's Dread. You haven't seen him, have you? He's kinda gone missing."

"Naw. Haven't seen you guys since that night. We went to a house after, remember? Awesome party. Lots of booze and drugs, some chicks. Good times."

"Yeah, said Earl. I remember that. We had lots of nights like that. It's a lifestyle choice."

"Sex, drugs and rock and roll, right?"

"Right on brother. Anything like that out here?"

"Not really. The biker scene is better down in Renton, same with the music. It's pretty quiet here. Police keep a lid on things."

"Fucking cops."

"You got that."

"How about drugs? Things are hot in our bars and we figure these rich kids out here have to get wasted now and then. You know any way we could score?"

"Maybe. What are you looking for?"

"Oh we're easy, anything to get high."

"I can make a call. Actually, I'll make a couple calls, check you guys out. Can't be too careful, right?"

"Wouldn't have it any other way. Go make your calls."

He came back a few minutes later.

"Okay, you guys are cool and my man can hook you up.

Did you drive or are you on bikes?"

"Bikes."

"That's no good. This guy's smart. He knows the cops are all over bars like this so he's a boutique dealer. Hangs out in upscale places and your Harleys wouldn't fit in at all. I can drive you if you want."

"Sounds good. Our bikes okay here?"

"No one steals from this place."

"Got it. Okay, let's roll."

Their new friend's name was Jake and he drove them into town in his Honda Civic.

"I hate this car," he said, "but I gotta work. I sell real estate and people buying houses don't like riding out to see 'em on a chopper."

"Understood," said Dex. "What you gotta do."

"Right."

"Where we headed?"

"Bellevue Square. Last place in the world the police would look for a drug deal. You okay with that?"

"No problem."

"I'd take off the doo rags if I were you. And I got some other shirts back there. We should throw them on, try to look normal."

"Makes sense," they said.

They walked inside the mall and Jake led them to Sharper Image.

"Buy something cheap. We just need the bag."

Dex bought a knife that wasn't cheap but he liked it. The clerk put it in a bag with Sharper Image on the side and they walked out. Jake led them to a Starbucks. They bought coffee and sat down at a table. Dex took out the knife, put it in his pocket and put some bills into the bag. He slid it to Jake who put it between his knees and counted the money. In a few minutes a guy in a suit came over, also carrying a Sharper

Image bag.

"Jake," he said, "good to see you. How's the real estate biz?"

"Not bad. You need a house?"

"Not today. Mostly I need coffee. This day trading wears a guy out. Mind if I join you?"

"Have a seat."

No one was around them so they could talk.

"I got what you ordered," said the day trader. Dex liked that term, "day trader" sounded so much more legit than "drug dealer."

"You got the money?"

"In the bag," said Dex.

"Mind if I look?"

"Help yourself."

Dex slid his bag over and the trader looked inside. He turned to Jake.

"You count this?"

"Yeah, it's all there."

"How do we know your product is good?" asked Earl.

"Take my bag over to the men's room and try a line or two. See what you think."

Earl looked at Dex, who nodded.

He took the other bag to the men's room. The other three drank their coffee and talked. They set up a way to make contact. Earl came back and said, "I'm buzzed. It's good shit."

"Okay," said the trader. "We're good?"

"We're good."

He got up and left.

# CHAPTER 44

FOR WEEKS DREAD experienced way too much time on his hands. Now he had company and he was enjoying it. At night they were sleeping upstairs in the penthouse and he found he could sleep the whole night through, something he hadn't done in years. They'd let him play bass and he made it a point to play longer and longer until they got used to it. One day he broke a string. On purpose. It wasn't hard to do, as the bass they'd found for him on eBay was old and so were the strings. They bought him a new set and let him use wire cutters to cut off the ends. They were very careful to take back the wire cutters, the old strings, and the ends but they didn't notice him cut two short lengths off the old strings and pocket them.

He'd never learned to pick locks, but he'd seen the basics on TV cop shows. You needed a tension spring and a thin tool to work the tumblers. He figured the thick end of the E string could work as the tension spring and the thinner end of the B string could be used to work the tumblers.

At night, when they turned off the lights and left him to sleep, he spent hours trying to pick the padlock on the cell door. In the dark, he had to reach through the bars, and some nights he would nearly weep with frustration. When he was done he stuck the wires into gaps at the top of the cage because nobody checked ceilings. He got so he could get two or three tumblers set, but the fourth one defeated him until one night he got it just right and voila! The lock opened.

His next problem was what to do. He could escape, tell the police and get Bernadette, Monte, Nails and Lucy thrown in prison. Once the cops saw the cell it would be a no brainer, but oddly enough he found he didn't like that option. He'd come to know them and they'd treated him with kindness, even Bernadette who had every reason to hate his guts. Maybe his meditations had warped his mind. He didn't know.

His other option would be to escape and not tell anyone. But that would mean he would never see Bernadette again. It was really weird, but he didn't want that.

His third option was to sit tight and see what happened. He could always get out and he was curious to see how they'd solve the Eddie Moon problem. There was no hurry, as he was eating well, Nails was teaching him how to box, Lucy was letting him work with her on the elevator problem, and he wasn't sure he wanted to go back to his old life. It was really kind of crappy when he thought about it. Living in a ratty apartment, playing music in hellhole bars, dealing drugs. No, he decided, he'd wait awhile and see what happened.

Every night he would pick the lock to make sure he stayed in practice. Some nights he would open the door and walk around the room. In time he got more adventurous and checked out the rest of the floor. He knew Eddie Moon was behind the door next to his but he had no urge to go in. Moon would just want him to pick his lock and set him free and that wasn't going to happen. Moon was notorious among Dread's bar crowd as a homicidal maniac. Scary. Dread had no desire to meet him and even less to set him free.

So he kept his lock picking secret and waited.

# CHAPTER 45

IT SHOULD NEVER have happened. A couple weeks later, Dex and Earl drove back to the Square to meet the day trader and get more product. That same day, Bernadette and Nails drove there for supplies. Even with them being in the mall at the same time the chances of seeing each other were extremely slim. Fate plays with us all.

Dex and Earl were pulling out of their parking space when Bernadette and Nails walked out of the mall. Dex saw her first.

"Hey Earl, look at that woman."

"Yeah, she's hot. What's she doing with the old black guy?"

"Look again. Recognize her?"

"Nope, do you?"

"Look at the way she walks."

"Okay, I can do that. I like watching hot women walk."

"Still don't recognize her?"

"Wait a minute! You think that's Bernadette?"

"I'm not sure. She looks like a Bellevue version of Bernadette. I've never seen her in anything but jeans, but it sure looks like her."

"Damn. It could be. What'll we do?"

"We can't do anything here. I say we follow them. See what we can find."

"Okay, they're getting in that tan Toyota," said Dex. "Keep driving slowly and you can pull around into their aisle."

"Got it."

They gave Bernadette plenty of room as she drove the Toyota back into town and they watched as she pulled into Grant Tower's downstairs parking.

"We can't follow them in."

"Right. I'll drop you off in front and you go in. Check the elevators. If there's one in the basement, see what floor it goes to. Finally, we're going to find that bitch and maybe she'll lead us to Dread."

Dex got out of the car and strolled into the busy lobby and over to the elevators. He watched the numbers above them both and saw the one go to the basement, then up to the fifteenth floor. He checked the register of offices and saw just one name for the fifteenth floor. Monte Grant III, Private Investigations.

"Can I help you, sir?"

Startled, Dex turned around. It was the guy from behind the front desk. He wore a uniform but didn't seem too threatening.

"I think I've got the wrong building," said Earl.

"Okay, let me walk you out."

They headed to the front door and Willie, the security man, held it open.

"Have a nice day," he said, happy to get the scruffy guy out of the building.

Dex walked back out and got into their van.

"Got 'em," he said, "fifteenth floor. She's seeing a private detective! Why the hell would she do that? What do we do now?"

"Somehow, we got to get up there, find out what's going on. Any ideas?"

"Not now. Let's go snort some inspiration and see what we can come up with."

"Good plan. I think a lot better with a little buzz on."

# CHAPTER 46

BERNADETTE MEDITATED. She'd done it every day for months in Dread's room, sitting on her cushion, counting her breaths. Dread was in his cell and he was meditating too. He was not going to let this woman show him up. Surprisingly, his meditations had changed. He no longer used the time to curse the world or plot revenge. It was just too much work. Bernadette had told him about mantras, where monks would have just one or two words they repeated over and over in their minds, trying to get to absolute purity of thought. Dread thought that was stupid, but in time he'd thought it would be funny to meditate on his favorite two words. "Fuck you." He was in the middle of a session when he thought of that and he almost burst out laughing. What better way to cut through this maharishi bullshit than to meditate on the ultimate curse? So that's what he'd done for three months.

He'd been amazed to find himself getting deeper and deeper into the words, going from rage to frustration to sexual acts to a complete song he wrote in his mind with those words as the title and the hook. In time, the words became softer, more peaceful, and now they were meaningless, just jumbles of letters he repeated with each breath. Before, they'd been loaded with anger, emotion. Now they were his mantra. He never told Bernadette.

He could feel himself changing, and he resisted violently. He found himself looking forward to meals with Monte, Lucy and Bernadette, and he liked it when they listened to his opinion. He liked it when he was able to help them with the taser that took out Eddie Moon. Was he becoming a wuss? The question nagged at him. Sometimes he looked at Bernadette and realized she was quite beautiful. She was no fashion model, but beautiful in an athletic sort of way. She moved with grace. He'd always thought of her face as plain, kind of skinny and pale, but now that she was off drugs and eating better she looked way more healthy and alive. *No sense dwelling on that*, he thought. She was forever lost to him. He kept meditating. Smiling as he repeated his words. Ah yes, Grasshopper, the Fuck You Monk.

LUCY AND I WERE the ones who spent the most time with Eddie Moon, and I figured it would take about 175 years to change him from an astoundingly evil person to one who maybe just committed assault with intent to kill. Lucy and I talked about it, and he was indeed like a tiger. His nature was to rip things apart and kill them. I could see no reason at all to talk to him, but it was our plan so we did it.

Lucy regarded him as an exhibit. She just stared, amazed that anyone could be that savage. I talked to him but I don't know if you could call it a conversation.

"Oh good," Eddie said, "the zookeepers are back. You gonna throw me some raw meat?"

"Maybe. Or you could have some burgers. That's what we're having."

"Okay. I'll take one. You got fries with that?"

"Yeah, we got fries and a coke."

I slid them through the bars. Burger and fries in cardboard, Coke in a paper cup.

"You guys are all heart."

"Enjoy."

"What's the news on the street? My guys coming to get me and destroy you people?"

"I don't think your guys miss you at all. You brought all kinds of unwelcome attention. They're probably happy to be doing business without that."

"Someone will come. Or one of you will rat out the others. Trust me, I know criminals."

"Yeah, but we're not criminals. We're just ordinary folk."

"You're kidnappers for Christ's sake. That's a federal crime. You're criminals looking at years in the slammer."

# CHAPTER 47

NOT EVERYONE IN Eddie's organization was happy. Sam Dropo, the new boss, didn't trust Eddie's boys, for good reason. They were like mini Moons, trigger-happy, vicious thugs who enjoyed inflicting pain and, of course, death. Dropo, sometimes known as The Suit, was trying to drag the organization into the future. Oh sure, he still ran drugs, protection rackets and prostitution rings, but he wanted them to make more money. And that meant streamlining the business. He wasn't above taking out competitors or authorizing force where he felt it necessary, but he was more of a corporate gangster. Eddie's old boys chafed under the new regime. They wanted their old boss back.

The only question was whether he was even alive. Chances on that were pretty slim. Most of the guys figured he was deep in Puget Sound wrapped in chains. But there was a tiny chance he was alive somewhere. If they could find him, they could re-take the gang and go back to their old, brutal ways.

So they suffered under the new boss and kept their eyes and ears open. Some of their eyes and ears belonged to cops, because no police force is totally clean and there were always cops on the take, even in the best of cities. One of the things they heard was that a task force was getting search warrants for the Grant Tower because Eddie was last seen going into it. Now there were doubts that he was the one who'd come out. It was hard to tell from the traffic videos, but he looked different, walked different. Had he stayed inside? Or had he driven away and been hijacked?

There was going to be a search. What if Eddie was in there? If the cops found him first, that wouldn't be good. Too much publicity, more heat on the gang, all in all a bad situation. Eddie's buddies decided to go in before the cops, get him if he was there, and sneak him out.

But they'd reckoned without The Suit. He too had sources, bent cops, and he too found out about the police raid. His thinking was the same. If Eddie was in there, it meant bad publicity, more heat from the Feds, and worst of all, Eddie. Deep in his heart Dropo knew he wanted Eddie to be dead. Disappeared forever. If Eddie was alive, he was dangerous. He would not be thrilled that Sam had taken over the operation and Sam was not thrilled at the prospect of torture and slow death. He had to get into that building first.

Dex and Earl knew nothing of all this. They just wanted to get Bernadette and force her to tell them where Dread was. They staked out the building she and Nails had driven into, looking for an opening. The weird thing was they'd watched the building where she'd gone to see the detective and she'd never come back out. The Toyota hadn't left either. What the hell was she doing? Was the detective her new boyfriend? Was she living there? They wanted to find out. If they could just sneak into the building, they could grab her, get her to talk and go find Dread.

Suddenly, Grant Tower was about to get very popular.

We knew the police would be coming, but we weren't preparing for a full-scale invasion by multiple forces. Our only goal was to make an entire floor of an office building disappear. How hard could that be? How hard could it be to get two elevators to skip a floor with nobody noticing? How hard would it be to change the directory downstairs without Willie noticing?

Piece of cake, right?

Lucy had been working on the fake elevator panels and was having problems. To eliminate the prison floor, we had to change my office floor to fourteen, which was simple enough, and we could change the number over my office door to 1401.

The penthouse floor became fifteen, but there were no numbers involved. In the elevators it just said, "P."

Our elevator panels had two rows of buttons. Odd numbers on the left: 1, 3, 5, 7, 9, 11, (no 13), 15. Even numbers on the right: 2, 4, 6, 8, 10, 12, 14, P. Her new panel put "P" over the fifteen button and set the fourteen button to stop on the fifteenth floor, my office. Lucy explained this to me and it was all I could do to keep my brain from exploding. It seemed simple to her. It was quantum mechanics to me.

She was confident she could build new panels with new buttons. It was at that point that Dread said he could help. I found his offer extremely odd.

"Dread, if the cops find Eddie they're going to find you too and you'll be free. Why the hell would you help us?"

"If the cops find us, that means Bernadette will go to jail. I can't live with that."

Bernadette stared.

"Are you kidding me?"

"No. I know I'm an asshole and that's not going to change. If I get out I'll probably screw up again. But I also know you're a mother and those kids might be mine. I can't let them throw you in jail. So I'll help."

"Bullshit," I said. "You're just trying to get out. I don't believe you."

"You don't have to. I can work in the cell and Lucy can test the panels. You've got nothing to lose."

We agreed he had a point.

Then we got lucky.

The Lone Ranger had his trusted Indian companion, I had my trusted homeless scout. Nails had spent the past few days on the street, frequenting his usual haunts, having breakfast with me on the steps, trying to pick up any info on what the police had in mind. We were getting nervous until one of his fellow beggars tipped him off.

"Hey Nails, what's up?"

"Nothin'. Just spare changing."

"Word is we shouldn't be around here tonight. Something's going down with the cops."

"No shit. Where'd you hear that?"

"Old George got rousted. You know him, got that good spot near the heating vent? They told him to clear out tonight and not come back till after midnight."

Nails knew the spot. It was behind Grant Tower, near the back entrance. My trusted scout could read the signs. He sneaked back into the building and warned us. Then he cleaned up and we prepared for a busy evening.

# CHAPTER 48

THE FIRST THING WE did was move the kids, Nails, and Lucy up to the penthouse. That way we'd all be set and ready for the big night. With their stuff upstairs we could turn my office back into a legitimate-looking business with Bernadette and me working late.

We gathered around Bernadette's desk.

"Okay," I said. "Lucy you slap on the fake elevator panels and office number. What about the stairs?

"Again," said Nails. "I don't see cops climbing fifteen flights of stairs. All we can do is lock the doors to fourteen and hope they don't go that way."

"Right. I'll go down and change the office registry in the lobby. When do you think the cops will come?"

"I'm guessing around nine," said Nails. "It would be too much of a hassle to deal with all the people in the offices. Does that make sense?"

"Sounds right," I said. "I can let them in to all the offices and they can search to their heart's content. Okay, let's get cracking."

DEX AND EARL HAD talked about what they should do and decided their best bet was to somehow get into the building in the daytime and find a place to hide. Then they could search at night, when the building was empty. Somehow, they would find Bernadette. It wasn't much of a plan, but it was the best they could come up with. The trick was going to be getting into the building and hiding.

They thought about a delivery of some sort. Computer parts, pizza, something along that line, but guy at the front desk was sure to ask who it was for and then call up to that office. Not good. They watched the building and as near as they could see all the guys dressed in suits could just walk in and head to the elevators. Neither one had ever owned a suit and Earl's neck tattoos would show over the collar of a dress shirt. Not a good look.

They decided that if Dex could get a suit, he could walk in, go up to an upper floor and hide. Then he could come down that night and let Earl in. Earl's brother was legit and worked at a Ford dealership. He was about Dex's size, so they called him, told him Dex had to go to a funeral and asked if he could borrow a suit and tie. It took some persuading. That afternoon Dex got the first haircut he'd had in years, along with a shave. Earl was surprised to see his rocker buddy actually looked pretty good. He felt a twinge of jealousy.

The next day Earl dropped Dex off a block away. He looked entirely different in his suit, black shoes, dress shirt, tie and a briefcase they'd bought at a pawn shop. Dex strode confidently down the street, entered Grant Tower, crossed to the elevators and punched the up button. Other people got on and pushed buttons for their floors. None of them pushed six, so he did and got off there. He was in a hall with office doors lining it so he walked, looking for a place to hide. He spotted a janitor's closet, walked in and found he could safely hide behind the door. He did so, sitting down on a box of supplies and taking sandwiches and water out of his briefcase. It was 3:30 p.m. and he was scheduled to open the door for Earl at 8:00. He watched Kung Fu movies on his cell phone with ear buds. It was boring. He wished he'd brought some Columbian to snort, keep him alert. Damn.

SAM DROPO KNEW the police planned to go in that night after office hours. He wanted Eddie found and eliminated before that. Epps was the guy. Epps was a renowned hit man, the best in the business, and Sam had briefed him on the job.

"Eddie might be in that building somewhere. We don't know for sure. If he is, you got to find him and take him out before the police get there."

"What about the body?"

"Let them find the body. We're better off if everyone knows Eddie is dead. What do you think? Can you do it?"

"If I can't, no one can."

Epps left. Sam sat back and lit a cigar.

JOEY FRANZ AND ROSS DELGADO, Eddie's trusted lieutenants, had been tipped off to the raid by their own bent cops and wanted to get Eddie out first so he could come back and take over the organization. The big question was how to get in, find Eddie and get him out before the police showed up. Their plan was a bit more primitive.

They walked into the lobby after the last of the office workers had left. They headed over to the guy at the front desk, shoved a gun in his face and said, "Where's Eddie?"

Poor Willie was dumbfounded and had no answer. They hit him a couple of times, but he still didn't know so they tied him up, gagged him and stuffed him behind the high desk. Then they took the elevator to the first floor and walked down it yelling, "Eddie!" This was their plan. They weren't deep thinkers.

Dex left the broom closet and went down to let in Earl. They walked to the elevators and headed for the detective's office. Odd. Dex could've sworn it was on fifteen, but the directory said fourteen. They got in the elevator and punched fourteen. There was no fifteen so Dex realized he'd been wrong.

EPPS WAS SURPRISED to find the lobby door unlocked and no one at the front desk. Weird. He'd planned to walk to the desk, shoot the security guy, hide the body and go look for Eddie. It made him uneasy but he didn't have a lot of time. Epps was a nondescript guy, fortyish, with thinning brown hair, clear glasses he didn't need, and catlike reflexes. He was lethal with any weapon. He walked in. He too had to figure out how to search the building.

He took the stairs to the first floor, cracked open the door and heard some idiots yelling, "Eddie!" in the hall. What the fuck? He let the door close and climbed up to three. He figured he could check out the first two floors after the bozos were done.

He opened the door on the third floor and realized he had no way of searching locked offices. But if Eddie was alive someone had to be guarding him and they wouldn't be sitting in the dark. He quickly walked the hall, looking for light coming from under any of the doors. There was none, so he went back to the elevator and pushed the up button. He got in and headed up to four. He would find his man.

Dex and Earl got out on my office floor and were stunned to see Bernadette sitting behind a desk, equally stunned. She was playing computer games, waiting for the cops. She pushed the send button on her phone and Nails and I got "They're here" text on ours. Odd, the police shouldn't be here for another hour.

She recognized Earl but it took a few seconds to realize the other guy was Dex.

"Holy shit, Dex, don't you clean up nice!"

"Hi Bernadette. Where's Dread?"

"How the hell should I know?"

"He headed out to meet you that night he disappeared and we figure you know what happened. You're our only hope of finding him, so just tell us where he is. We don't want to hurt you."

"I swear, Dex, I don't know what you're talking about."

"Goddamn it Bernadette, quit stalling. Just tell us where he is or we're going to have to get rough. I'd hate to do that."

"I don't think you should talk to a lady that way," I said as I walked out of the office behind Bernadette.

"Who the fuck are you?" exclaimed Earl.

"I'm Monte. Who the fuck are you?" I realized I'd come to enjoy swearing. Hey, you hang out with criminals and it rubs off.

Bernadette answered for them.

"They're Dex and Earl, Dread's band guys. They think I know where Dread is. But I don't."

"Well shit," said Dex. "This is getting complicated. Now we have to deal with an old guy and then get some answers from Bernadette.

"Two old guys," said Nails from behind them.

Startled, Dex and Earl turned to look. All that heavy bag work paid off. Nails caught Dex with a rising left hook that laid him out. I have to hand it to Earl. He got in a couple of big swings before Nails stepped in and caught him with two driving punches to the solar plexus. Earl bent over and an uppercut finished the job. Dex started to rise, and Bernadette clocked him with her purse. Apparently, she had some heavy stuff in it. Done.

"What do we do now, Boss?"

"We can't let the police find these guys."

"Yeah, and we can't get them out of the building."

Bernadette spoke up.

"Put them in the cage with Dread. They can have a reunion."

It sounded good to us, but we realized we couldn't get the elevator to stop on the prison floor.

"Shit," said Nails. "We have to use the stairs."

"We can't carry them, they're too big."

"The service elevator. Quick."

We were bent over, trying to drag Earl first, when a voice behind us said, "Just stop right there. Don't move."

Bernadette was looking past us and said, "Better do what he says, he's got a gun."

"Okay," said Epps, "stand up slowly with your hands in the air."


WE DID AS we were told.

"Turn around."

We turned around.

In front of us was a guy in a stocking mask, surgical gloves, dark clothes and quite a big gun in his right hand.

"We'll do whatever you want," I said. "By the way, what do you want?"

"Eddie Moon. I came to deliver a message. You wouldn't happen to know where he is, would you?"

"No," I said. "Do you mean Eddie Moon, the gangster? The one in the papers?"

"Yeah. And I don't believe you."

"Just then the elevator doors opened behind him and two guys came out yelling, "Eddie! Where are you?"

The guy in the stocking mask just shook his head and backed up so he could cover us all.

"Shut the fuck up!" he yelled.

Joey and Ross took one look at the gun and shut up.

"Get over there with the others."

They slowly raised their hands and edged over to us. Epps nudged Dex with his foot and he opened his eyes, groggy. He took one look at the gun and said, "What the hell?"

"You and the other guy, over there with the others."

Dex roused Earl and they managed to stand up and move over with us.

"Okay," said Epps, "I'm going to be quick. Who the hell are all you people? Let's start with you two.

"I'm Joey, he's Ross. We're here to get Eddie and he's going to kill you if you get in our way."

"Okay, mark me down as real scared." Epps laughed. "Next?"

"I'm Dex and this is Earl. We're here to rescue Dread."

"Dread? What the fuck kind of name is that? Who is Dread?"

"He's our bass player and lead singer. We're a band."

"What the hell does he have to do with Eddie Moon?"

"Nothing. We don't know who Eddie Moon is. These guys kidnapped Dread and we're here to rescue him."

"This is unbelievable," said Epps. "You guys kidnap gangsters and bass players?"

"Well," said Nails, "there's more to it than that. The bass player is a wife beater."

"Oh, that clears it all up!" said Epps, rolling his eyes. "Unbelievable. I'm in a bad movie here. Okay, kidnappers, who are you?"

"I'm Monte," I said. "I own the building."

"You're shitting me."

"No, it's true."

"I'm Nails," said Nails. "I'm a homeless boxer."

Epps slapped his forehead. "Of course you are. And I'm a flamenco dancer. How about you, lady?"

"I'm the one Dread beat up."

"You don't look beat up."

"It was three years ago. I was in prison after that."

"Of course you were. They always put people in prison for getting beat up."

"No I was there for punching out a cop who was trying to arrest me."

"For getting beat up."

"No, for beating up someone else."

"Of course. It's all clear now. Okay," said Epps, "this is just getting silly so we're going to cut to the chase. I could kill you all but that would be really messy and my employer would hate that. What's going to happen is one of you is going to tell me where Eddie is. Then I'm going to lock you up somewhere and deliver my message. We're running short of time, so quick, where's Eddie?"

We looked at each other.

"You're going to kill him, aren't you," said Nails.

Joey and Ross protested. "You can't let him do that! We came here to rescue him!"

"Shut up," said Epps. "What I do with Eddie is none of your business. But I need an answer quick so here's what I'm going to do. I'm going to shoot the lady unless someone tells me where Eddie is. If you still don't tell me, I'm going to go down the line until someone talks. As I said, I don't want it to get messy so why don't you tell me right now."

With that he put the gun to Bernadette's head.

"I'll show you," I said. "Put the gun down."

"Okay," said Epps. "Good choice. Now, I need a place to lock you all up. Any ideas?"

"You can put us in the cell with Dread," said Nails. "It's big enough."

"Okay," said Epps. "Now were getting somewhere. Lead the way."

We trooped out of the office and down the stairs to the prison floor. I pointed to Eddie's room.

"Eddie's in there, in a cage."

"Perfect," said Epps.

I led us to the other door.

"Dread is in here."

"Dread," he said, "what a stupid Goddamn name."

"You're right," I said.

"Open it."

I opened it, flicked on the lights, and we all walked in. Dread sprang to his feet.

"What the hell?" he exclaimed.

"It's a long story," I said, "you're going to have company. Lots of it.

I unlocked the cell door and we started to troop inside.

"Stop." said Epps.

He pointed the gun at Joey and Ross.

"You two stay right there. Don't move. The rest of you, inside."

"Okay," said Epps, "I'm guessing you two have weapons. In very slow motion, you (he pointed at Joey) are going to take out all your weapons and put them on the floor. Then you (he pointed at Ross) are going to do the same. Then I'm going to pat you down and if I find anything I'm going to shoot you. Understood?"

Ross and Joey did as they were told and between them they had three guns and a couple of wicked looking knives. Epps kicked the weapons over to the corner.

"Okay," said Epps, "in the cage."

Epps closed the door and locked the padlock.

"The keys," he said.

I gave him my keys.

"Any other keys?" he asked. Nails and Bernadette tried to look innocent but he was too smart.

"You two, turn out your pockets."

The did, and gave him their keys.

"Which one opens the door to Eddie's room?"

I showed him.

"Okay," you guys sit tight. "I'm going to have a word with Eddie."

"Do you need the key to his cell?" I asked.

"Not really," he said. "I just need a quick word."

He left. Bernadette spoke up.

"Lucy. He doesn't know about Lucy and the kids. If we don't show up she'll come down and rescue us."

"Or get shot," said Nails. "I've never met a hit man but I'm guessing that's what that guy is."

"We have to do something," said Bernadette.

"Well," said Dread, "we could leave."

We turned to him.

"How?" I asked.

He reached up to where the bars met at the top of the cage and took down his two wires. Then he edged through the mass of bodies to the door of the cell. Constant practice had made him skilled and it only took a couple minutes to unlock the lock. Bernadette stared at him.

"You could've gotten out any time?" she exclaimed.

"Well, yeah," he mumbled sheepishly.

She stared at him.

"Why didn't you?"

"I don't know," he mumbled.

She stared at him for a few moments.

"We have to talk," she said.

We got out of the cell, Bernadette, Nails, me, Dex and Earl. Ross and Joey started to follow but Bernadette said,

"Not you two."

It was then they noticed she'd picked up one of their guns and was aiming it at them.

"You know how to work that thing lady?"

"Well, it's a SIG Sauer P365 with offset double magazines.

I think I just pull this little thingy here."

We all stared.

"Bikers love guns," she said.

They backed up. Dread locked the lock and we left them there.

"I should get a gun too," he said.

We voted no.

"I need something," he said. "That guy's a killer." So he picked up his electric bass and followed us out.

We crept out the door and down the hall to Eddie's door which was slightly open. Dread and Nails crept to either side of it, with Dex and Earl, bewildered, backing them up. Bernadette stood across the hall with the pistol leveled at the door. Inside we heard voices, Epps and Eddie. Eddie sounded like he was bargaining, trying to buy his way out. Then there was a gunshot, muffled by the soundproofing. Then there were two more. We waited. The door opened and Epps, unsuspecting, stepped out.

Bernadette stood in front of him with the SIG Sauer pointed at his forehead. Startled, he froze. Nails chopped his gun hand down and Dread leveled him with a guitar blow to the head, proving the bass could be used as a weapon. Teamwork. We tied him up with duct tape. I reminded myself that when all this was over we were going to need more duct tape.

"Okay," I said, "we have to figure this out. The cops are going to be here soon. What's our plan?"

"We can't let them find the jail cells," said Bernadette. "If they do, we all go to prison."

"Right," I said. "But we have to give them Eddie and this hit man. How do we do that?"

"We can't move the body," said Nails, "but how do we keep the hit man from spilling everything? He could tell the cops about the prisons and put us all in jail."

Just then Lucy came out of the stairwell.

"I got worried," she said. Then she looked at all of us. "What the hell?"

"Are the kids okay?" asked Bernadette.

"Yeah. They're asleep and I've got the monitor. What's going on?"

"No time to tell you," I said. "Those cells aren't welded together, right?"

"Nope. The sections are fitted together and clamped.

"Can you dismantle them?"

"Sure, but I need allen wrenches. They're in my toolbox next door."

"How quickly can you take them apart?

"With help? We could dismantle them in maybe thirty minutes apiece."

"An hour. We don't have that long."

"We can split up," said Nails. "Lucy can undo the clamps while we take away the bar sections."

"Okay," I said. "Lucy, Eddie Moon is dead. Can you take down the cage around him? We can't move the body so we'll have to leave the floor. Is that possible?"

"Actually," she said, "that makes it easier. We won't have to unbolt the floor. Can we do the same with Dread's cage?"

"Sure. The plywood covers the floor bars so that works. Dread, I continued, "did your guys come in their van?"

Dread looked at Dex and Earl. They nodded.

"Are their instruments in there? Please say yes."

Dex nodded. "They're there."

"You guys want to help us out or get involved in a murder investigation?"

It didn't take them long to figure that one out.

"Okay, we'll get those cages down. Here's my key card. You guys go get the van, drive it downstairs and get all your drums, guitars, amps, speakers and load them in the service elevator. Hopefully we'll have the cages down by the time you get up here. Bernadette, you go take care of the kids. Dread, you go take the fake panels off the elevators. We'll let the cops go wherever they want."

"Boss," said Nails, "you're forgetting something."

"What's that?"

"Eddie's guys. Ross and Joey. They're locked in the other cell."

"Damn," I said. "Any ideas?"

We all paused. Nails came up with the answer. We went back to talk to Eddie's guys as Lucy went to work on the clamps.

Nails and I grabbed the other pistols Epps had left lying on the floor. Then we covered Ross and Joey, unlocked the cage and gave them a choice. They could hang around and get interviewed by a ton of cops at a murder scene. Or they could try to make it down the stairs and sneak out the garage. I put their life chances at fifty-fifty. There was no way they'd go back to the organization now that Eddie was killed.

Just to be sure, we forced them to the other room and took pictures of them standing over Eddie's corpse, shaking hands. We figured they'd either be in prison or out of the country by morning.

# CHAPTER 49

THE POLICE CAME a little after nine. Lots of them.

Nails was at the front door, dressed in Willie's security guard uniform. Willie was up in the penthouse being attended to by Bernadette. We'd called 911 when everything was ready, so it was kind of a clusterfuck when the cops responding to the call arrived with sirens blaring, just as the task force was gearing up to silently surprise us and do their search. Nails was waiting with the door open and yelled that there was trouble on the fourteenth floor. Someone had been shot.

The cops and task force all rushed to the elevators and it took a few moments to sort out who was going up first. They spilled out onto the fourteenth floor. Lucy and I were waiting for them.

"This way," I called, and led them to the room where Eddie's body lay on the floor, the jail gone. On the floor across from him lay Epps, arms and legs duct taped and tape over his mouth.

A detective ordered everyone to stay back while he rushed over and checked Eddie's pulse. He was careful where he stepped, as there was lots of blood. With a bullet in his head and two in the chest it was pretty obvious Eddie was dead but he had to make sure.

"Holy shit," he exclaimed, "this is Eddie Moon."

He turned to the guy taped up on the floor.

"Who is this?"

"The killer. My security man was on patrol when he noticed this door was open. He approached and heard the first shot. He rushed in just as this guy was shooting twice more. He got him from behind with his baton. Then he found the duct tape and wrapped him up."

The detective looked at the hitman on the ground.

"Do you know who he is?"

"Not a clue. He's wearing that stocking mask. His gun's over there. Nails kicked it away and we haven't touched it"

"Nails?"

"Nails Norrison. He used to be a boxer, now he works security."

"Okay," said the detective, "let's see who we got."

He undid the tape over the mouth of the hitman and lifted up the stocking mask.

"I don't recognize him," he said. "Must be from out of town."

Epps started yelling.

"This is bullshit! Eddie was kidnapped! He was in a cell! This is all a frame up! You can't prove anything!"

"Well," said the detective, "we've got you. We've got a gun. We've probably got powder residue on your clothes. We've got you wearing a mask and gloves. You got to admit it looks pretty good for our side."

"It was a kidnapping!" yelled Epps. "I can prove it! There were two rooms with cages! Go next door! They got a guy named Dread locked up in there! He'll tell you!"

The detective looked at me.

"Dread?" he said.

"I know. Weird name."

"You got a room next door?"

"Yes," I said.

"I want to see it."

"You do that," said Epps. "These people are crazy! Eddie was in a cell here and the guy next door is in a cell too."

"I don't see a cell here," said the detective.

"I swear Eddie was in a cell. Check next door. That guy will tell you and you can see the cell for yourself!"

The detective had the police untape Epps and cuff him, then we all trooped next door. I opened the door and we were hit by a blast of noise. Inside, Dread and his band we're set up on the raised plywood floor where the cell had been, drums pounding, guitar wailing, bass thumping and Dread screaming out a song. I motioned for them to stop.

"Who are you?" asked the detective.

"We're Chains of Destruction, the best biker band in town," said Dread.

"What are your names?"

"This is Dex, Earl's on drums, and I'm Dread.

"Dread?"

"Yeah, I know. Kind of a bogus name. I'm thinking of changing it."

The detective smiled.

"Good idea. We got a guy here who says you were kidnapped and being held in a jail cell."

Dread laughed.

"The guy's looney tunes. Mr. Grant rents us this room to practice. It's soundproofed so it doesn't bother anyone. There's another band that uses the room next door but they're crap."

The detective looked at me, looked at Epps, and said, "Okay, take this guy away and book him. Murder one. But he should get a medal for taking out Moon. Life isn't fair."

Epps was yelling as they took him away.

# CHAPTER 50

THE POLICE TOOK all our stories. We were helped when one of the old cops recognized Nails and said he'd seen a couple of his fights. He got an autograph. I made a mental note to create a post of head of security and hire Nails. Then I made another mental note that I shouldn't hire a binge drinker as my head of security.

The cops taped off the crime scene and the investigators went to work. We spent two hours going over our statements and then trooped upstairs to the penthouse. I brought out a bottle of twenty-one-year-old Balvenie scotch I'd been saving for a special occasion. If this wasn't special, I didn't know what was.

"Nails," I said, "is this going to set you off?"

"Hell if I know, Boss, but who cares?"

I had no answer for that.

Bernadette was talking to Dread.

"You could've escaped. You could've put us in jail."

"I know. I sure wanted to. But I couldn't do it."

"There's no way in hell we're getting back together."

"I know that too. I just didn't want to see you back in prison."

"Okay. So we're good?"

"If I stay straight for awhile, could we have coffee sometime?"

"Okay," she smiled, "but I'm bringing Nails. One false move and you're a goner."

"I still think I can take him."

Nails laughed.

"In your dreams."

"I'll miss the meditation," said Dread.

"I'll tell you what. You're sober now. You stay that way, come to meetings with me every day and we can meditate too. But I'll always have Nails with me. Deal?"

"Deal," said Dread. He didn't tell her about his mantra. Some Buddhists wouldn't understand.

## The End.

Made in the USA
Monee, IL
24 July 2020